An Emirati writer with a master's degree in Management and Marketing from the Sorbonne University – Abu Dhabi, in the year 2010.

He started heading toward the field of literature and poetry to present his thoughts and opinions, and he used to participate as a collaborating writer during intermittent previous periods in the world of Emirati journalism and magazines, and he wrote many literary works on different subjects (short story, poetry, novel, self-development).

He participated in book fairs such as Sharjah, Muscat, Riyadh and continues to be creative in the fields of writing, composition, and poetry, especially free poetry, and lyrical poetry.

While his interest in writing stories and novels took a major direction for his current intellectual interests, he aspires to become one of the most eminent writers in the Arab world during the coming period as he translated his literary production into English, French, and other living foreign languages.

To those dear to my heart, through whom I feel the breath of my life, my family and loyal friends, without whom my existence would have no value, in a world in which I woven my most beautiful literary paintings, From their faces, the world begins, and from their laughter, I hear the purity of their souls. To my family and dear children, I send heartfelt kisses loaded with the nostalgia flowing over the years…

Obaid Mohamed Aljeraishi

Lotus Bouquets

AUSTIN MACAULEY PUBLISHERS™
LONDON * CAMBRIDGE * NEW YORK * SHARJAH

Copyright © Obaid Mohamed Aljeraishi 2023

The right of Obaid Mohamed Aljeraishi to be identified as author of this work has been asserted by the author in accordance with Federal Law No. (7) of UAE, Year 2002, Concerning Copyrights and Neighboring Rights.

All rights reserved. No part of this publication may be reproduced, stored in a retrieval system, or transmitted in any form or by any means, electronic, mechanical, photocopying, recording, or otherwise, without the prior permission of the publishers.

Any person who commits any unauthorized act in relation to this publication may be liable to legal prosecution and civil claims for damages.

This is a work of fiction. Names, characters, businesses, places, events, locales, and incidents are either the products of the author's imagination or used in a fictitious manner. Any resemblance to actual persons, living or dead, or actual events is purely coincidental.

The age group that matches the content of the books has been classified according to the age classification system issued by the Ministry of Culture and Youth.

ISBN – 9789948785828 – (Paperback)
ISBN – 9789948785835 – (E-Book)

Application no: MC-10-01-5022362
Age Classification: 17+

First Published 2023
AUSTIN MACAULEY PUBLISHERS FZE
Sharjah Publishing City
P.O Box [519201]
Sharjah, UAE
www.austinmacauley.ae
+971 655 95 202

All appreciation to those who stood beside me during my literary career with unlimited support, moral and material encouragement.

All gratitude to those who harnessed the means of success for me so that I could stand firm in the face of the difficulties and challenges that I faced by making the most of their advice.

Beginnings

At every dawn, the sun rises and casts its golden rays to herald the advent of a new day, and it does not differentiate between an urban city or a rural one; what matters is that in any of the big cities, people do not know much of its details. When you take the look of a flying bird, logic will not give you any explanation. For the wide and narrow streets, nor for the human crowds or even the cars, where the roar of activity emanates from their engines. All people, without exception, within sight are mere stories that move in a violent debate with the hands of the clock, fighting circumstances to conquer them.

Some bewildered faces are rigid, and there are some tears sitting in tired eyes, whether they are old men or women, or even young men and children. For everyone, the world at the horizon line does not end at the sky, as much as it ends at the line of care and ends are carefully governed.

As for the morning sun, it is, as usual, sneaking out of the window of this girl's room, who was destined by fate to live in complete prosperity with all its details and linguistic synonyms. Richness has undoubtedly imprinted its distinctive and striking icons on her life.

(Ibtisam) was not just a spoiled girl in the usual metaphorical sense, for sure, as she is fond of an instinctive madness in drawing, and in her heart she does not secretly like being a rich girl from the upper class, and the funny thing is that she basically did not choose anything from this life.

But it is time in its strange and shocking development, as it is often not interested in sensitive hearts, or so Ibtisam thought at the beginning of thinking about the true meaning of life and its accompanying living conditions.

Since her delicate childhood, she has not tried to be anything but a gentle, polite girl.

She did not bear in the features of her face what indicates the breadth of grace and what expresses the breadth of prosperity.

People have strange thoughts about those who live in the comfort of life, sometimes they are wronged by their negative impressions that accompany some of those who are superior to people with money.

Are jealousy and envy adorned with garments of hatred?

However, (Ibtisam) was gentler than what many of her loyal friends think, and she did not bear sharp or repulsive features.

A girl whose voice is barely audible when she speaks in tones of modesty. She moves from the inspiration of her feminine instinct. Honestly, her mother, Mrs. Fatima, had a clear role in her upbringing. It made her immune from the concept of a stereotypical life, which in turn is consistent with a family that may be described as wealthy.

The childhood of the young woman (Ibtisam) shows melancholy memories that come back to her whenever the need arises, but they are distinct and influential. She was affected by the frequent absence of (Ahlam) her twin sister, with her aunt, to the extent that her teacher noticed that the way she drew faces was truncated and incomplete, and she often drew incomplete things. So, the principal summoned her to her office, and asked her to see her mother tomorrow morning for an important, urgent, and fateful matter.

At first, the Mother thought, when she heard the strange request, that the teacher would complain about her tender daughter because she is silent most of the time and often presents her ideas through drawing, and in a different notebook that does not belong to the homework notebooks but rather a strange one that does not correspond to other notebooks at all.

Certainly, the Mother was betting on the content of the complaint as she walked to the teacher's office in her head ringing the bells of frustration non-stop, but unfortunately, what I heard from the teacher as soon as the Mother settled on the black chair in the office was strange, as she took out a set of papers of different sizes for her, it has truncated drawings, and the objects in it are incomplete and sometimes distorted.

The Mother was hit by a thunderbolt that disturbed her thinking for a while. It was unfortunate that she held her tongue at first, as she did not know who these strange, terrifying drawings were for. It is clear that her daughter (Ibtisam), whom she knows, had never been caught before on any occasion drawing such horrible shapes, but the rug of astonishment extended when she knew that it was her daughter, and with this sad news, she now understands the real secret behind her summoning today.

So she began to think that the girl might have quarreled with one of her classmates or done similar reckless behavior, but she returned from the consequences of that hurtful thought because she realizes how kind she is and her lack of inclination to conflict with anyone, as she is most of the time lonely, tolerant. And she loves to bypass all events.

There, the teacher realized, based on her experience, that the Mother is confused, and she does not know the secret of this morning summoning, and in a matter concerning her kind daughter for sure, she indicated to the Mother that the drawings are for the girl (Ibtisam), and she noticed a while ago the prevalence of this artistic approach in almost everything she draws, so it does not come out of the colored pencils in one complete shape.

This is a very important sign that heralds, without any doubt, the existence of a psychological crisis experienced by a child of her age, and as long as nothing is complete in the imagination of the child, this also means a terrible emotional void that has its future negatives and a loss that cannot continue to be overcome. Under the pretext that the girl is often silent, does not merge in any way with the surrounding world around her, and does not even complain about anything.

Under the influence of the difficult and constrained astonishment of the shocked mother's thinking because of what she hears about her daughter and the irrefutable evidence, she only tried to surrender to the intelligence of this teacher and her suspicious yellow looks, so she had already interpreted these drawings in an explanation that proves the existence of a psychological crisis in the life of her dear daughter.

It seems and is certain that her tender aunt (Ibtisam) could not protest at all on the day the family moved her twin sister to her grandmother's house and to live with her aunt, who (God) deprived her of the blessing of childbearing, in the hope that this aunt will share with the little girl some of the lost motherhood.

Soon, the shocked mother gathered some of her mental fragments and began telling the teacher the whole realistic story at once, which answered all her questions about what she saw from her daughter's strange drawings, so the teacher advised her, in turn, that her sister come to stay at home, because this would restore the lost balance to the girl, which she needs at this age.

Here, the Mother (Fatma) took out the booklet of the daughter (Ibtisam), which she used to record in it in a pattern of thoughts, so she put it on the desk in complete calm and coolness.

Her movement talks about a very important matter that she intends to reveal immediately, then she spontaneously tells her details of the silent nights of this girl when she wakes up some nights from her sleep in order to record something like impressions or night diaries.

When the teacher took the little pink booklet and began to read carefully and focused, some signs of confusion and anxiety appeared on her round face. A lot of verses of admiration for what was written appeared on her cheeks, forcing her to continue and refuse to stop reading silently, muttering with her lips in a whisper.

With an involuntary movement, she removed the chair and went to embrace (Ibtisam), who was standing in love and tenderness, despite the young age of the girl.

She was good at revealing but also commenting on the details of her day, but she was keen to convey to the Mother some reassurance, as perhaps the girl tends to draw and write because she does not dare to express her complaint by commenting on the absence of her only sister.

It is certain that if her absent sister returned to live with her, concepts would change and her habits would change successively, even if she does not see in this habit anything that indicates anxiety or apprehension and suspicion.

The tender-hearted girl seems to have merit in any case, and what she draws shows her hidden abilities. And who knows? Perhaps in the coming days it may be different.

At this moment, the Mother sympathized with her daughter and was greatly grateful to this teacher called (Hessa), who indicated that there was a talented girl in this family, so the Mother asked her permission to leave immediately with a smile and left her office.

And she was seeking to devise a plan with which she could retrieve (Ahlam) her daughter's twins; her only goal is to end her suffering and completely close the open door to the painful past.

When the father (Saad) learned from the Mother about this visit and its details, he suspected that their daughter might be psychologically tired, but he did not want, despite his apprehension, to seek medical help directly. In order not to burden the innocence of a girl at this age or even scare her.

But he was thinking carefully about what was beyond this transient crisis on the surface of the family, especially since his inclinations and dreams of his twin daughters were tending to imbue their souls with masculine qualities that would help them in the future to face a time when difficulty would have a place in their lives. His concerns escalated as he heard about the rest of the school visit events.

Conflict

(Ibtisam) realized with her intellect that the Father's apprehensive portrayal of her was her ordeal on the day she obtained her high school certificate, as her sister most likely finally responded to her father's dream and lived through her ambition to become a doctor, but (Ibtisam) from another angle was not intellectually compatible with such a proposition of desires, through the fullfilment of the dreams of the family, and in particular the dear parents.

Her old teacher's bet has been fulfilled, and her talent for drawing and writing has crystallized, but the difficult question remains looking for answers in light of the current circumstances: how will she convince a family belonging to that time with all its pressures, and only sees one side of the world, which is the struggle for wealth, where the work that it never ends, and no one ever admits failure.

And when she tried to reason with her Mother (Fatima) out loud, she was referring to the concept of giving inherent in her personality, as she has something like a moral responsibility toward young girls.

She wants to teach them and follow the path of her old teacher, this intelligent lady who realized her crisis from just simple, innocent drawings that did not agree with her age at the time.

This model is what some girls need. She is an expert teacher who is good at capturing simple details. To establish and educate according to successful educational standards,

Of course, its ultimate goal is to create a generation that is beneficial to itself and its society, and that human meaning stemmed from Ibtisam's suffering with loneliness, as her sister had left for her aunt, her father was busy in the financial world, and her mother was part of a work machine that took most of her time.

The Mother (Fatima) used to hear what her daughter told her, and she felt that two wings were emerging from her sides out of her excessive happiness at the maturity of her daughter, which seemed to be manifested while she was talking about her ambitions.

However, she realizes that if she intends to pursue a teaching profession, she will never satisfy her father's plans, who long ago formulated the shape of his daughters' future and paved the way for them.

Ahlam's submission to his wishes will only be a point of weakness in favor of Ibtisam, who will then appear like a rebellious girl against the ambitious father's plans, whose ideas are not flexible at all.

People often no longer think in the same way as his daughter, who wants to crystallize her humanitarian giving in the form of work that does not bring profit only and works for it, as much as she wants through it to help girls find their ambitions and, most importantly, facilitate the means to achieve them.

One day, during an hour of contentment that the Father feels, the Mother (Fatima) takes the initiative to throw her daughter's ambition in the way of the father and begins to refute in front of him the details of the dream that controls his daughter. She reminds him of her childhood setbacks. This step confused her, and she knew that half of her heart and soul were absent from her.

The continuous work that consumed the merchant's father did not enable him to follow up on what his daughter was thinking about, so he did not know that she was different and had her own talent in expressing herself, since from an early age she had embraced pen and paper, so her mother was not the only presence in her life, but what she used to write and draw in her old notebook as her real mother, who did not deprive her of her sister under human reason, but it was very painful for her innocence.

It seems difficult for a person's conviction to change with just a personal decision or for his desires to intersect with another desire, and from whom? It is his daughter, whom he truly loves. Perhaps he traveled with his thoughts, re-navigating his daughter's ambition with his abilities and data. A man whose only job is to collect money, then move it into a new business,

Here, he thought carefully about investing in education in a model school that presents the educational message in a better and more effective way.

When (Ibtisam) learned of this desire from her father, she was not motivated by its content, or refused it outright and irrevocably, even if the desire was embedded within the psyche of the shrewd merchant. According to him, he sees education as a message that must be presented in an ideal and successful manner, capable of producing a different, truly educated generation. And consistent with others who learn in any part of this vast world.

But inside her conscience, along with her idealism, according to her point of view, she found a huge difference between education and commerce, as she was absolutely certain that her father was very stubborn, even when he was responding momentarily to her aspirations. He never forgot his ideas as a trader before anything, and his renewed convictions that do not calm down to achieve profit by avoiding loss and its forms.

Education and medicine for those like (Ibtisam) two issues that should not be subject to the concept of commerce, but they fall under its direct influence, and what spoils the two is that tendency toward investing everything human without looking at the results, as some people may be harmed from where we do not know and do not calculate.

In medicine, we invest in people's instinctive need to enjoy good health and try to get them out of the circle of pain, aches, and infection. In education, we trade on people's tendency to obtain knowledge and get them out of the circle of ignorance to the shores of science and creativity to build civilizations and advance peoples.

However, the victory over the father's conviction in accepting his stubborn daughter's enrollment in the College of Education remains a victory, if not decisive for him. At least he may allow her to pursue an ambition that she already loves at the present time, but he is also convinced that the coming days may change concepts.

After graduation, something else may happen that is not taken into account, if she marries a person who believes that her talent is greater than being imprisoned under the pressures of life and its unstable, volatile circumstances and its mighty mills that crush the delicate, simple, and peaceful hearts, which always strive to achieve victory for their humanity, in order to wash away and purify from society's hateful materialism.

In a coincidence that was not frequent, the girl (Ibtisam) gathered her father at the breakfast table, so Ibtisam tried hard in various ways to put her desires in front of him in the form of a conversation so that her father would understand from her what she chose for herself.

It is fortunate for her that her father, who has extreme materialistic thinking, had in his heart a reasonable space of humanity that could be built upon, until she gets rid of the shackles of his business ideas.

Indeed, tendencies of sympathy for her thoughts moved in him, and it was clear that he was weak about her features that reminded him of his late mother, as his daughter (Ibtisam) is a miniature of her paternal grandmother, gentle, kind, and affectionate.

He asked her if this was her decision, and she nodded in the affirmative, so he patted her on the shoulder as he was about to get up. The spontaneous movement had a good effect and a veiled encouragement in its content.

On the other hand, the human features on the face of the Mother (Fatima) gave her hope that life, no matter how fluctuating and changing, could go according to the wishes of her sensitive daughter.

Her father is not a merchant like the others, and he is not like that group that is fully prepared without alarm or fear of the possible fate to throw their human hearts out of the human equation.

This father can stand up for his humanity whenever he wants, even though his features are often unfair to him. He does not want to show the tenderness of his fatherhood. He is afraid that someone will accuse him of spoiling his two daughters. She remembers when her mother told her a story that proves what she thinks.

The Father had an old friend called (Abdul Rahman) who for years believed that her father was heartless, for he was a man who could not cry under the influence of any human reason at all, and he was petrified of feelings.

On one of the family trips, where the bonds of friendship were strengthened beyond imagination due to the homogeneity between (Ibtisam) and (Ahlam) and between the daughters of Mr. (Abdul Rahman), the great surprise was that when the Father saw Ibtisam, he kept embracing her and saying: (You are the one who proved to me that your father knows how to cry). The girl was young and did not understand at the time the signal sent like lightning from his words to her.

At that moment, her father laughs at the situation as he remembers the details of this fateful day for the whole family. He carried her like a madman to his car, almost falling out of fear and tears covering his eyes. She ate a piece of candy, which caused excruciating pain in her weak stomach, and she still suffers from this pain sometimes.

At the end of this story, Ibtisam realizes that her father is not a cruel man, as it appears from his behavior and the expressions of his always grim face.

Perhaps he himself is a victim of the system of personal characteristics that gave him this harsh model of feelings. It seems that he is an overbearing father, but on the contrary, he is kind and loves her, and he is terrified if something bad happens to her.

She also remembers, from her old childhood heritage, another situation on the day her young uncle hit her, and she knew how much he loved and respected him, so she did not like to complain to her father at the time.

She is absolutely certain that her uncle will never be punished for doing so, and that stems from the excessive love shown to him that everyone noticed and felt; even a stranger would not miss these feelings between the two brothers.

Her father used to see this rude uncle at times as a good omen for them. Because of his birth, many doors of sustenance were opened to him, and clouds of good deeds began to fall on their family like rain irrigating their barren lands. Rather, his presence brought prosperity and the increasing prestige that the family had experienced until this moment.

But what the girl (Ibtisam) missed at the time was that her father was observing his younger brother's arrogance when he punished her with excessive, authoritarian cruelty for a mistake that never required this humiliating deterrent punishment. While tears flow down her cheeks, she wails in silence and weeps.

At that moment, she left, holding back the rising groans of grief in her crying, while she was trying to broadcast what happened to her quiet father, who suddenly erupted like a volcano, surprising her with an angry call to come to him quickly.

And soon he called her uncle at the same moment, exaggerated his rebuke, rebuked him with harsh words, and pointed out that he was her second father after his departure, and he could never treat his daughter in this cruel way.

Memories of the Faculty of Commerce are still firmly in her mind, and a year or less before (Ibtisam) graduated, which she chose to enter as an attempt to catch the stick in the middle, a great argument occurred between her and her mother (Fatima), as soon as she told her that the issue of private and model schools was a field for the expected investment is not the desired goal.

For her personally, this does not constitute the largest and most important part of her human aspirations, while her mother indicated that her father does not absolutely respond to the desire of any of his daughters, so he must put the data of his thinking and perceptions on everything.

After these signals, sent in a logical sequence, her mother began to accuse her of being confused and not knowing what she wanted and desired.

Wait!

Her mother told her how happy she was with this approach when she heard what he was thinking about it, so what has changed? Or is the truth that nothing has changed?

She was just thinking about it, and she did not want, through what she sought, to appear as a girl who practices disobedience that she does not like toward her father and his sometimes-disturbing desires.

After this diverging argument, which is not devoid of kindness and romantic feminine literature, the conversation between them stopped on the indication that it is not wise for them to precede events, as many unexpected things may happen in the last year before graduation, as the movement of the fates always brings goodness, and no one knows what it carries. his coming days,

Here the Mother got up with a semi-smile on her face that hides secrets behind her as she looked at her daughter's expressions.

Although (Ibtisam) finished her studies, she still lived in a state of stillness and lingering, observing things with piercing eyes full of apprehension. So what will happen to the events in the coming days?

She is not driven by her father's dreams, nor does she want from another angle to work in his company, especially in the field of accounting, the subject of her specialization.

However, after the passage of two consecutive years in which dreams were sometimes repressed and struck, and at other times happy and fortunate, her twin sister (Ahlam) was able to succeed in medical school with merit, but she did not have the right to self-determination.

It has no choice but to be led unwillingly or to feel the satisfaction marked by coercion and without thinking to meet the aspirations and desires of the father, who plans their life together from an early age and bears their concern alone.

It is a good coincidence that the celebration of her success was followed by her engagement party to a young man from the family's surroundings; he is the son of the notable who smiles at life with the spirit of ambitious youth, while on the other hand, (Ibtisam's) joy remained incomplete and truncated with feelings, as she was apprehensive about something, while everyone was joyful and living a full-fledged joy. The two girls finished their education, and the time has come to implement their future plans with all courage and without delay that spoils enthusiasm.

But for her, this relative calm was like a storm that destroyed dreams before she was born.

It is, in fact, a feeling that suddenly appears and takes over her thoughts, and even disturbs her, making her life difficult. Even in her sleep, she dreamed of him crouching on her breath, suppressing her happiness and crushing her, so what can she do about this Father's domination with his thoughts?

Even as she received his precious gift, which was postponed until her sister (Ahlam) finished her studies, the congratulations accompanying the gift did not escape from a public indication of this father's desire to sit with his daughter, so that they plan together the shape of their perceptions of the private school that he seeks to establish, and it is certain that it will undertake the matters of its administration.

The night of the celebration was the longest and most difficult night for her psyche. She tried hard to fall asleep, but she could not, so why is sleep so stubborn and quarrelsome?

Tomorrow is a difficult day by all intellectual standards, and she will sit with her father and hear from him what contradicts what she dreams of. Managing the school is a huge responsibility in which the difficulties are manifested on a daily basis, and the responsibilities will grow and burden her.

Inside her, she knows that she will not spend all of her time running after the mirage, as much as it will kill her captive desires to continue practicing a job that she loves and adores with all her being. So how will she be able to convince her mighty father of her thoughts, and from where will she get her logical justifications through which the mind of this stubborn and steely Father will soften ?

Alone with her confused self, she wonders what is the successful alternative that, if mentioned, she will be able to practice her hobby with flexibility without hardship, and on the other side, she can achieve something like profits, which in turn will rejoice the mentality of the Father (Saad), that experienced merchant who only recognizes what he believes in. And that this life is relentless, as it does not build the dreams of the laggards at all.

The next day, the kind girl (Ibtisam) knocked on the wooden door, and she was allowed to enter, and it seemed that her father was not alone in his office, so she offered him to come back after he finished his engagements while looking at him smiling, but he unusually asked her to sit, so she seemed confused at this moment. She completed her smile, and in herself, the windmills of questions were spinning, and unfortunately, no answer was evident to her.

She sat with her eyes looking at the old brown table, and she saw a set of papers, drawings, and maps.

These engineering drawings and plans are an initial drawing of the model private school. And her details, as her father dreamed of.

The Father (Saad) had the wisdom to detect the confusion and turmoil that appeared clearly on the smiling, gentle face of the girl, and soon he asked the strange man to leave and ordered him to think about the matter slowly. He promised to resume the study of the project later in the coming days and to give this subject the bulk of his interests and nothing else.

Here, (Ibtisam) realized that the matter was not related to her at all and that this strange man in the blue suit had come for a reason related to her father and his various projects, but he ordered her to sit and wait for a while, and the word wait in some situations may mean waiting and psychological calm to regain lost wisdom.

Could he simply play cat and mouse with her at this fateful hour?

It seemed to him that he was ignoring her presence as he was turning over those papers in silence, reading and glancing at his daughter out of the corner of his eyes from behind the golden-rimmed glasses.

Then, suddenly, he pounced on her and asked her directly, with a smile on his face as if it refused to leave his lips: (What is wrong with you, my dear, my little girl? As if you are not betting on our next step?)

Her thoughts scattered at once; she did not know how to answer his sudden question that turned the scales; her calm became just an opportunity for him to pounce on her, but she regained her confidence.

And out of nowhere, courage came to her, and she made a double effort to be able to explain her opinion and put forward what she intended to do on her night, which was the longest night that she had passed.

At that time, the Father (Saad) realized that his tender daughter (Ibtisam) was no longer a little girl.

In her voice, there was the self-confidence that her father felt while smiling and still looking at her from behind the glasses as she spoke to him:

"- My dear father... I understood from your old speech, the day I joined the College of Commerce, that education is an important human message in every sense of the word.

- From my personal point of view, it should be presented in an ideal and elegant manner, and this meaning cannot be overlooked, as I have no reservations about it.

- But inside me is a painful feeling that my presence at the helm of such a project might kill my desires, which I was encouraged to do one day by the smile of satisfaction I saw on your face.

- I argue that education as a message may seem beyond my capabilities, but I am not imploring you to never forget this idea.

- However, it is really necessary to complement it, and by that I mean to develop it in a way that contributes to the establishment of the ideal private school and to entrust an organization from the family or from outside it to manage it so that it can play its desired role in society."

With the intelligence of the shrewd merchant, the happy Father (Saad) realized from this beginning that his tender and talented young daughter (Ibtisam) would not be able to head this project that had a huge amount of responsibilities and importance. So that he can see how his daughter will think if she finishes her education?

But at the same time, he fears for her the deadly emptiness of ambitions and the demise of the feeling that she is responsible for an activity that makes her life a true and realistic message that triumphs for her existence.

In addition, the stereotypical image of a girl who loves to draw and lives among his colors with her brushes and her thoughts running through his paintings does not encourage him to leave his daughter for her talent to manage it however she wants, waiting in silence and stillness, and waves of suspicions throwing him while he thinks.

Realistically, he was trying to find out from his daughter's detailed speech what indicated an alternative that would make him satisfied with her and reassured him of her brilliant future, so his features remained in a tyrannical rigidity that he was able to really confuse her.

But she impersonated the audacity to the end and did not stop expressing her opinion, as this may be the last round for her, in which perhaps there will be a huge profit or loss.

In fact, she did not indicate her shocking and outright rejection of the idea of establishing a model school according to her father's business specifications, but she made a clear and decisive statement that she wanted to invest her talent in the field of commerce, but with her own ideas without interference from anyone, even if this person was her dear father.

Her heart guided her, after long deliberation and continuous prayers, in which she beseeches God to guide her to the right choices, so she arrived in the spirit of the word (message) that she heard from him to offer him to establish a school, in which she would be part of its management team, without contradicting her other dreams, and she said that without hurting her father's dignity and causing him embarrassment.

Absolute stillness was her father's trait after he listened to what she said, and he became terrifying and frightening to her. He faced her bold words with complete silence, as his eyes did not move, as rigid as a stone, and with features that did not herald anything more than a disguised rejection behind calmness or an implicit resentment that he hated all the ideas she presented to him.

Is it just stubbornness?

Although she had told her father that she had asked (God) in her prayers to inspire her with the right path and guide her to this step, she does not know what comes after all this silence.

She was so afraid that she said in a whisper that he could almost hear: (I'm sorry if her father happened to find in her words what sounded like the ravings of a girl without any experience).

The idea of becoming, at this age, the owner of a project that belongs to her alone is completely unpalatable and completely rejected.

And to be honest and truthful, this silent Father did not bear any of her thoughts, unfortunately. The man's experience enabled him to anticipate well, so his silence was only to repeat the maneuver in another way.

It is clear to him that his daughter (Ibtisam), whom he knows well, will not give up her ideas so easily and surrender. He raised her on that and instilled in her the principles of struggle.

She really would not have the ability to challenge him with stubbornness; he was only waiting for her to find a convincing alternative solution to what he proposed to her regarding investing in education.

From his point of view, the school is important and influential and even presents the message of education in a way that makes the experience a model that is easy to build upon, so that the experience may spread and achieve unexpected successes.

But he did not see from her a complete abandonment of the idea from its roots, and this was the new thing that he did not expect from her. However, the girl dear to his heart did not go beyond the idea of school from the ground up, as he thought, with her first smiling appearance, as she entered his office room, walking with steady steps, as if she was counting the time. She did not want him to move forward. An apprehension confused her movement. She felt the feelings of her father sending them to her through his vacillating looks between contentment and rejection.

She wants the whole family to contribute to the management of this model school, or to choose a body that supervises it and monitors the quality of education, its inputs and outputs, and through which it is provided, but what really pleased the Father is that the little girl never got the idea out of her dreams and never rejected it.

However, after the end of the legendary family meeting, Ibtisam continued to laugh throughout the following days whenever he remembered her features as she left her father's office. she did not feel complete reassurance or of deep, crippling anxiety. The Father's features may be confusing to the point of bewilderment, but she is not totally rejecting this idea. She believes that there is absolutely nothing that makes her father reject her ideas openly and decisively. Especially since he will always be by her side, supporting her.

There also appeared to be a whispered side conversation between the mother and her father, telling him the developments of (Ibtisam), who did not leave her room or seek to go out with her friends.

Ibtisam slept during the day and at night dipped between her papers, as in the old days, as she did not leave either drawing or writing, and she used to push her writings through her e-mail to websites and platforms.

In fact, the Father (Saad) did not comment on the hadiths he heard coming from the mouth of his wife (Fatima), the companion of his path and struggle, nor did he give any clear indication that his thinking crystallized as being sympathetic to her ambition, although he never thought of obstructing what she dreams of. He just wants to verify what you are seeking before issuing his final and definitive opinion.

It was really a game of patience, and her father (Saad) did not know any developments that occurred to her since they talked about the school or her alternative dreams during the past week, and he did not speak about this issue, neither from near nor from afar, until he noticed that she did not appear at the dinner table, and he really felt her frequent absence.

So, with this new and strange behavior, did Ibtisam escape from confrontation? He says to himself: *(It is impossible for my daughter to escape from confrontation)*.

He did not ask her mother to move; in order to ask her to share food with them, so he decided when he finished eating to pass by his daughter's room. When he reached the door, he knocked on the door once, and when she opened it, he spoke without looking at her and said decisively: ("If you do not insist on what you heard from me, then take this sheet.")

Ibtisam did not speak, but extended her thin hand and took it gently and smilingly. The paper belonged to a senior employee who used to work in an important bank.

(Ibtisam) did not know how she received these brief words! She actually shut her up, but at these moments she sensed signs that she did not know her father.

Fatherhood is a complex case, most likely, moving on the shores of love that is abstract and devoid of any goals, and sometimes there are no justifications for it so that the explanations get lost and drown in a sea of suspicions!

This Father with rigid feelings respected her ambitions and never dared to transcend them, considering them mere idealistic dreams that would not bring profits comparable to the profits of his other commercial activities.

Rather, the word commercial did not fit her spirit, and he was only testing her sincerity to her ideas.

It has become certain that his perceptions of this project are much greater than what she thinks, as the first batch to complete this ambitious project will not be according to what you want and hope for.

She is passionate without any doubt, and she can evaluate the ideas that will be presented to her, as she wants to achieve victory for what she believes in.

**Are the hands of the clock deliberately delaying the clock?
Or am I not arguing with reality, so I flee into illusions...**

Ordeal

The movement of destinies was between ebbs and flows in the life of the tender young woman (Ibtisam), and it was somewhat strange in its events.

She was not betting in the most extreme dreams that the dream would end with the death of the father, who was not complaining of any illness. Rather, health was measured by comparing it to her father's health. How can health have a title carved on his face?

On a special evening, her mother did not return home at her usual time, and it seems that she was late due to a great controversy that her uncles had initiated some time ago about some financial matters that had been pending for a long time.

She thought her mother's house was quieter than her father's, but when she came back relatively late that July night, she bet her father would leave his room to admonish her for being late.

It was a night that (Ibtisam) did not know from which hell this night came to her and how this night laid its foundations on the happy coasts of Ibtisam, and even the fates of this night messed with her.

Her sister (Ahlam) got up from her sleep terrified, continuing a cry that seemed to have been released during her sleep, so she got up to complete it in the space of her room, and fear had seized her body; and in her eyes, a beam of alarm illuminated the darkness of the room.

And because she does not know the deep sleep that abandoned her to be replaced by the inevitable anxiety, she was unable to close her eyes and continue sleeping, so she explored the details of the nightmare that touched (Ahlam) and disturbed her sleep.

She felt a sudden panic that she could not explain, and her mother, from her position, stood at the door of her father's room with strange stability, holding the door handle, and there was nothing to hear except the air coming out of her chest, rising and fading like the waves of a hurricane.

And there is one person she did not find crowding the scene: her father, who told them to calm down because he is under the influence of a temporary fatigue that will pass and it is not necessary for them to call the family therapist this late at night, and his face looks pale and his voice is broken, and you can hardly hear the words scattered.

The next morning, Ibtisam was not sure that she had fallen asleep. Rather, she heard the voice of her mother (Fatima) calling her continuously and non-stop, so she immediately went jogging. She was talking to her with great concern and in a conversation in which sentences were incomplete and the words truncated, most of which she could not understand. She tells her that she smells the smell of death that will break into the house, and she feels a lot of fear and terror, so she embraced her immediately and started kissing her head.

There is a sound of death whose steps you can almost hear, and when I asked her to go to summon (Ahlam), she was hiding a state that was greater than the meaning of anxiety and terror. There, Ibtisam heard her father's voice calling her, asking her to bypass (Ahlam) and to inform her mother that he wanted to have breakfast. His desire to eat is a source of optimism from everyone and sows reassurance.

The breakfast preparation was finished, and her mother went to fetch her father from his room. (Ibtisam) did not notice her mother's long pause in front of the door of the room, but she closed the door and returned to ask them to eat. As soon as their father gets up, he will eat his share of the food.

But when Ibtisam's eyes rested in her mother's eyes, she did not see her eating. Rather, tears were falling profusely, and wailing was trapped in it; to settle in front of her as conclusive evidence of something big that has really happened.

Soon (Ibtisam) jumped from her chair and began rushing like a madwoman into the room, while her sister followed her. They found that their mother's talk about the smell of death that she smelled had become a tangible reality, and that sound meant that it had come into their house.

He stood staring at the silent Father, filling the room with a crowd of gloomy details, calling out to him in a loud voice, but he did not respond. The call was repeated to no avail, so she started crying with her sister.

The accident of a Father's death in this way was death in its meaning, which Ibtisam understood and realized after that. Rather, the truth in the guise of detachment is that everything died with the death of her father, who opened a wide door to the uncertain unknown. If it was not difficult, then at least it would not be devoid of a disturbance in thinking and a life turn upside down for quite some time.

With the death of the Father, the viewer could closely feel the amount of grace in which his family lived and how the days turned quickly and the destinies turned their mills.

Who would object to life's crises when they turn it upside down, but the central crisis in people's lives is not always easy to link to money and happiness?

There are specific crises that may occur. Crises speak out in bitter mockery of money and its owners when money stands helpless to get its owner out of difficult situations.

And these are only turning points that only require a strong will and insight that can contemplate the details and rearrange things as they were and will be. For life to continue to achieve its meaning, that simulates logic or almost reaches it.

The big, luxurious house and that upper floor, from which only a window appeared, draped with blue curtains with golden threads hanging down, concealed a room with bewilderment.

In this place there is a girl from this time, a time that the old people of her late father's age describe as a difficult time.

Thus, the circumstances of the tender young woman's tragedy were not normal, but rather one of her negatives became that she preferred, with the passage of time, to solitude, to drink the cups of her loneliness, she still wanted to look for any opportunity to appear; in order for her to succeed in finding a sympathetic friend who possesses the characteristics of a sister, instead of her sister, who could not bear life in its developments, so she left to complete her studies abroad.

To be honest, the travel of her sister (Ahlam) with her husband abroad was a difficult turning point in the life path of (Ibtisam), where the Mother's stagnation and her escape from her feelings appeared, and it became evident after the death of the Father, and it was so pressing that it caused confusion for everyone who spoke to her.

Perhaps the Mother took the method of escaping from her feelings: a theater in which she plays her new tragic roles with grace and good management?

It is that stalemate in the feelings that used to make her feel afraid for her mother, who seemed to have indications that she had not escaped from the shock.

Even the entry of (Aisha), her old friend, or, to be more precise, her intrusion into her life, was not helpful. The (Aisha) model of friendship does not mean the same meaning due to the different personalities. The young woman (Ibtisam) is not, of course, similar to her friend (Aisha) and never will be, whatever fates have played with them.

Perhaps she thought for a moment that the old friend (Ibtisam) and she, after the death of her father, would be more independent than in the past, with her feeling of complete freedom at last.

Certainly, Ibtisam has, from her inheritance, what makes her able to establish any activity that might provide a distinguished job for her friend (Aisha), and why not take advantage of this opportunity? This will not spoil the friendship between them, and she will not lose anything if she tells her about this in a timely manner.

And this, if it happens, will not shock at all (Ibtisam), who can instinctively analyze the real reasons that prompted her friend (Aisha) to enter her life now, but she needs someone to be present in her life as an echo of the details of her diaries instead of being alone with the blackness living in the shadow of whispers.This affects her life as a whole.

It was clear how much (Ibtisam) suffered from a state of imbalance in accepting life. Despite the presence of the whole family by her side and the wide and diversified network of relatives around her, everyone continued to shower her with kindness and tenderness, which would sometimes hurt her and make her feel the enormity of the sudden and shocking loss of her father at the same time.

This stage that followed the death of the Father (Saad) was one of the most difficult stages that the tender young woman (Ibtisam) lived through, as her mother (Fatima) seemed lost in life, losing the sense of her taste, which changed to bitterness that she swallowed regularly every day, as if it was a medicine for an incurable disease that requires non-stop. The fact that her sister (Ahlam) traveled abroad with her husband contributed to deepening this.

It also seems that new, completely unexpected legal developments have taken place, which have relatively affected the family and its savings. There are some financial arrangements that the Father, in turn, had drafted in anticipation of the moment of his death.

It seemed strange at first, and (Ibtisam) could not explain it with an appropriate explanation, especially since the shock of the sudden death was greater than any attempt to explain what happened, and logic was lost in the clutches of worries and sorrows.

She did not see signs of prejudice, but he felt a strong sense of belonging to the family, and he did not want, under the pretext that he did not have a male child, to put matters under the influence of greed, which might shock (Ibtisam) and her sister through the way the family deals with the matter of the two daughters and the share of each of them from the Father's great wealth.

The strange thing is that the bereaved mother was still in a state of shock, as the will that the husband left was clear and unambiguous, so when arranging the papers after the death of the Father, she showed an extreme feeling of abandoning the money, as there was no money mentioned with the absence of her husband from the stage of her life, she lost her soul through his separation, so she became a person who is ascetic to life.

Also, in the same session in which the will was recited, she decided to leave to (Ibtisam) and (Ahlam) her share of her husband's inheritance, even if through buying and selling, and it seems that (Ahlam) at this moment had decided to leave the country and leave, so nothing appeared on her indicates gratitude.

To be honest, her features were more neutral than those of (Ibtisam), who was shocked by the extremist talk about materialism and the calculations that she hates to delve into.

With the passage of time, the waves of confusion had hit Ibtisam's life and even stormed all her perceptions of the family's current situation, especially after the family completed the model private school project without giving Ibtisam a role in it as she had requested.

The sad thing is that all these feasibility studies and preliminary preparations were carried out by her father.

This behavior did not achieve the meaning of the apparent dispensation of Ibtisam's family, as much as it was a clear indication of the occurrence of a rupture, or at the very least that with the death of the Father, everything is over and family relations are lost, covered by the winds of oblivion.

On the other side of the river of social life, the Mother (Fatima) did not comment on this step. Rather, she was seized by an unusual state of bereavement, declaring herself satisfied with what had happened with her husband's family. She did not show any resistance, which is simply immediate surrender.

Rather, she was also grateful to her late husband, who did not think for a moment that he would break her heart with a new marriage experience, despite her many preoccupations and her attachment to social life, as time was her sworn enemy.

He could have fathered a son from another woman, inheriting his name, his wealth, and his complex and many diverse commercial activities as well.

The Shift

It was not easy for (Ibtisam) not to contemplate the new situation created by the tragedy of the Father's death. Rather, whenever she thought about the situation of (Ahlam), who left everything behind and accompanied her husband to travel, she felt a strong pressure on her soul, which did not hide her frank accusation of her only sister of abandoning the family at a difficult time.

This circumstance required them to rally around the distressed mother, who seemed to be completely broken.

As if time rushed backwards, and (Ibtisam) returned to the personality of this autistic child, who draws faces incomplete and objects distorted, as a shocking expression of the terrible loss and emotional emptiness that she was suffering from, especially when her sister (Ahlam) is in the bosom of her sterile aunt, on whom she practices lost motherhood as much as possible. And her tireless attempts to play this role considering the loss of hope.

She admits that the weight of the days and the details that resulted drained a lot of the balance of her resistance, so she seemed ascetic, as if she had completely stopped following her ambitions and dreams that were admired by her father despite his reservations and rejection of them at times, but now she surrenders to her fate for no known reason and finds no alternative. For her life, that seems to have stopped.

(Aisha) became her closest friend to her during this period, despite her belief that does not leave the certainty that the personality traits of her friend cannot give her full faith in their friendship, as she does not understand the true meaning of the word friendship as understood by (Ibtisam), who was raised on its impact and lived its lofty meanings between her family walls.

It seems that the friend (Aisha), whom she has known for years, is nothing but a complex case of anticipated apprehension and obvious anxiety. Rather, her looks were always full of secrets; although she belongs to a family with a good financial standard and may be described as living under God's protection, she does not know the concept of contentment with what the movement of its destinies accomplishes so that it is grateful and satisfied with its livelihood.

Perhaps she lacks confidence in herself and her abilities, even though she is on the standards of beauty. The human eye cannot surpass her because she is beautiful and evokes feelings before the senses. There is no greater evidence of that than what Ibtisam remembers from her explanation of the failure of her first engagement to an ambitious young engineer with a brilliant future. But for her, this is not enough at all.

She remembers how she immediately claimed that he was a shaky young man who did not trust himself. So, he left because he simply couldn't get a pretty, attractive girl to walk next to on the road.

She probably believed in this sense the day Aisha saw him coming out of a supermarket and walking past his new blonde fiancée.

As described, she was of average beauty, perhaps a few degrees below average.

Her self-confidence has become too much for everyone, and (Ibtisam) indicated to her in scattered conversations full of advice that beauty is really feeling confident, but the girl's other qualities are the touchstone on which her life is based, and the most important thing is her success in this life without relenting; the important thing then is to achieve ambitions in any way.

It seems that the friend (Aisha), whom she has known for years, is nothing but a complex case of anticipated apprehension and obvious anxiety. Rather, her looks were always full of secrets, although she belongs to a family with a good financial standard and may be described as living under God's protection, but she does not know the concept of contentment with what the movement of its destinies accomplishes so that it is grateful and satisfied with its livelihood.

Perhaps she lacks confidence in herself and her abilities, even though she is on the standards of beauty. The human eye cannot surpass her because she is beautiful and evokes feelings before the senses. There is no greater evidence of that than Ibtisam remembers from her explanation of the failure of her first engagement to an ambitious young engineer with a brilliant future. But for her, this is not enough at all.

She remembers how she immediately claimed that he was a shaky young man who did not trust himself; So he left because he simply couldn't get a pretty, attractive girl to walk next to on the road, she probably believed in this sense the day Aisha saw him coming out of a supermarket walking past his new blonde fiancée, As described, she was of average beauty, perhaps a few degrees below average.

Her self-confidence has become too much for everyone, and (Ibtisam) indicated to her in scattered conversations full of advice that beauty is really feeling confident, but the girl's other qualities are the touchstone on which her life is based, and the most important thing is her success in this life without relenting; The most important thing for her is to achieve ambitions in any way.

The biggest conclusive evidence of the credibility of what Ibtisam feels toward the friend (Aisha) is seeing her sad mother, because her father was rich in every sense of the word and he could carry out another marriage project that would bring him a son.

But he overcame a desire aroused in the eastern man, and it was certain that he loved her, or perhaps she gave him one of her convincing features, which made him sure and certain that he would not find a woman who would understand and comfort him like her mother.

Immediately, Ibtisam realized that there is no greater foolishness than confronting others with their mistakes harshly, as this may cause them annoyance and may even hurt their dignity in a miserable and inhuman way, despite the signs of her mother's discomfort toward her friend (Aisha) from the first impression and her awareness of the deep difference between the model of her daughter and her friend, who never hesitates in achieving her ambitions without caring about the price paid.

However, these impressions did not put an end to this friendship, which was originally founded on the meaning of fellowship. This made (Ibtisam) unable to create a rift that might be characterized by intensity and gave her great energy to be patient and formulate justifications for any ideas that might be shocking, and Ibtisam experienced many shocks from her friend regarding many issues.

One morning, Ibtisam received a call from Mr. Kamel, her father's friend, whose name was present on the paper her father wrote in his handwriting. The day he realized that his daughter would not interact with his project aimed at establishing an exemplary school for distinguished education, and how could she forget this name when it was entrenched in her memory, but rather carved with a chisel the events of time.

It was clear that the man's waiting indicated anticipation of the end of the mourning period, and he wanted it to come to him as soon as possible for training in the bank that manages an important banking sector in the system of trade and economy.

How much that invitation brought about a volatile weather in which confusion extends, which contributed to her confusion, as she was either close to approval or rejection or not paying him any attention.

Perhaps she had the certainty that asks about the feasibility of working now because what she got from her father's inheritance would help her complete her own project.

And when she wanted to think aloud with her mother about that matter, she found that she did not need to work for sure, and her answer was healing for her, and for the same reasons that Ibtisam gave to herself.

But she does not have the audacity of her father to enter the market with a business of her own, as her idealistic ideas may seem to have a clear rivalry with her ideal world.

But when she brought the matter up to Aisha, her eyes widened with joy, and she encouraged her to dare to implement this step immediately and even told her, when things settle down, to find a place for her in the bank as long as Mr. Kamel is a close friend of her late father.

Rather, (Azzam) gave her encouragement and useful advice from her point of view that working in the bank may give her vision the breadth she needs to be able to read the market and its requirements, an informed reading that may help her one day to complete her own project, whenever she decides to leave the bank and establish her life on conditions that are consistent with her old and renewed ideas.

Indeed, several days after the phone call, she went to meet Mr. (Kamil), and the meeting was full of events and memories that took their share. She realized with confidence that this decent man was not just an ordinary friend of her father, but they had a friendship close to a degree of human depth.

He did not want from the beginning to burden her with conversations and advice. Rather, he asked her to forget all that she had learned from accounting rules and to leave herself to Mrs. (Salma), the responsible and important employee in the bank, to train with her.

He advised her to focus on everything she says because she has a lot of experience, as she has been working in the bank for nearly ten years, and her personality is distinguished by her desire to teach sincere people who really want to learn.

The relationship of the young woman (Ibtisam) with Mrs. (Salma) has become fit to be the relationship of a girl with her mother, as this woman is approaching her fifties, relatively calm in character, sober in thinking, smiling slightly, and with a strong physical structure.

She is a widow, like her mother. Her son is a young man who invested the reward he got from the company his father used to work for and established a private farm in it, located on the southern side of the city, producing many plants needed by pharmaceutical companies.

The idea was surprising, especially for the young woman (Ibtisam), who saw that this ambitious young man was thinking outside the box, and it was certain that his mother had an important role in completing this infernal idea.

Of course, he is happy to have a mother who helps him plan and organize his life with her experience in the financial and trade environment, but is she also the one who plans his own life similarly?

The hours of training begin with the hands of time running, so the days go forward as fate wills them to be. Some exhaustion invades the weak body of (Ibtisam), and she often talks with her mother when she returns home.

She admits to her that the duration of the training period that she went through with Mrs. (Salma) was a world crowded with details and experiences that appeared from every line she read, but in the crowds of these days she forgot (Aisha's) desire to join the bank.

In her heart, she feels the embarrassment growing in her thoughts. She was aware that the obsessive nature of her friend would directly accuse her of forgetfulness and indifference.

But at the moment she saw fit, she presented (Aisha) to Mr. (Kamil), who welcomed the idea and asked her to coordinate with Mrs. (Salma) to participate in the implementation of the training sessions.

Abstract facts do not give themselves easily to the searcher for the truth. At this stage, she saw from (Aisha) another image that differed from the images that had crystallized in her mind since childhood and whose events extended to the years of university study.

In fact, the more you get close to her, the more you discover new things, as if this friend is a magic box in which there are wonders of the human soul, which makes her wonder: *(Is this really my friend)?*

Aisha seemed to be very demanding, but she also wanted to enter the life of Mrs. (Salma) and not just learn from her and take from the heritage of her long experiences.

When (Aisha) learned that she had a young son, an agricultural engineer, she began to practice some rude behavior with the kind lady Salma, who certainly did not need these practices at all.

What was surprising to the young woman (Ibtisam) was the abundance of pampering, rather than the humiliation that Aisha does, and this is also what Mrs. Salma felt, as from time to time she collides with her almost reckless thoughts, her behavior, and some of her comments that do not come in accordance with the whims and beliefs of the expert lady.

However, Mrs. Salmi was victorious for her kindness, so she transcended all these dramatic scenes, and she interpreted the matter as an expression of the ideas of a certain generation that differs from her generation in all respects.

The important turning point in the relationship of these three parties occurred on the day (Aisha) was appointed to the bank, and the desire latent in the heart of Mrs. (Salma) was to protect the tender young woman (Ibtisam) from her friend's revolution if she preceded her in the appointment. She would think that by doing so she would take over everything. Jealousy has a fire; if it ignites, nothing can extinguish it except the inevitability of revenge before the inevitability of defeat.

As for Mr. Kamel, his astonishment was faint and motionless, to the point that he did not care about the matter because of his blind confidence in Mrs. Salma.

It is clear that she has a respected point of view regarding what she recommended, even (Ibtisam), based on her experience with her friend, she thought about it in the same way.

However, the hidden part of the desire of the official (Salma) was to keep (Ibtisam) with her in the sector she runs; therefore, it was necessary for her to intensify her training and to give her everything she needs to be a successful employee who really deserves to be part of this important banking sector. Which is concerned with financing operations and accounting feasibility studies needed by any person who wants to invest in any private commercial activity.

As for the young woman (Aisha), she did not think about her next new step, but rather thought within herself that she is more distinguished than her gentle, dreamy friend and that she has gained the trust of the kind lady (Salma) with all her merit, which is evidenced by her interaction and enthusiasm in the training sessions, but she regrets bitterly. Then she said:

("I still have a long way to go to prove myself.")

And she began, as usual, advising her friend in a clear, arrogant voice that she should be patient with Mrs. (Salma) until she learns from her, and often (Ibtisam) drew colored smiles on her lips for these pieces of advice, which are almost vague smiles that carry many meanings of pity for her owner, who unfortunately sees things only from the angle of themselves without looking beyond their personal perceptions.

Over time, Ibtisam soon realized that her friend, Aisha, had a weak personality despite her courage. She only practices these stubborn behaviors to manage this weakness in thought.

She is strengthened by the rejection of what is definitely stable, until she establishes her imaginary difference through that system of strange behaviors.

Likewise, Aisha does not deserve a sudden, shocking reaction from her, which may translate into a rupture and an end to a friendship that spanned for years, but at the same time, she fears Aisha's continuous interference in her life, believing that she is more understanding and aware of things.

Where Ibtisam finds from Aisha what indicates Aisha's guardianship over her actions through an arbitrary, coercive intervention that she does not deserve from her at all.

There is no doubt that these personalities who provide advice are easy to fall into many problems, even with the people closest to them, and (Ibtisam) is not weak or helpless.

Ibtisam was the one who stood up boldly against her father's wishes when she graduated from high school. So, she is a person who understands the limits of her independence and knows what she really wants.

It seems that Mrs. (Salma) was aware of these meanings with her acumen and wisdom, and perhaps from the first sight she saw (Aisha).

It is strange that this meaning was manifested as the light of the morning on the day she held a limited celebration of her appointment at the bank. On that day, Mr. (Kamel) came to participate, in the presence of (Ibtisam), (Aisha) and the official, (Salma), who invited the guest.

Despite the limitedness of the party, everyone was happy except for the young female employee (Aisha), the only person who was necessary to be the most cheerful and happy.

Aisha was confused, as if she had committed a flagrant crime, and she looked at everyone with looks filled with confusion and anxiety that build their threads on her thoughts crowded with emotions and sweat pouring out, and she wiped it with white handkerchiefs that did not leave her hand wherever she went.

And in this particular situation, Mrs. (Salma) was of the intelligence that enabled her to read her emotions clearly, so that she asked her: ("Were you waiting for us to invite someone else to join us in the celebration?") So the answer was more silence and confusion, and looks that were not devoid of anxiety, as if she was searching for an answer in the straw of suspicion. Her tongue did not help her, as she was already stuttering, confused to the extreme limits of loss.

Perhaps (Ibtisam) did not pay attention to the sudden, direct question, except when she remembered the son of Mrs. (Salma), who at least did not come to see him either, even as an acquaintance, but it seems that her friend (Aisha) apparently has other goals, so she thought carefully to seize the precious opportunity in order to give that young man a look with a taste of promise or a desire to communicate, even remotely, at the present time.

The young woman (Aisha) could not control herself, so she tried hard to collect her thoughts. She realized at once that her tricks were exposed and that this lady called (Salma) was not a naive woman. In order not to understand the secret behind this state of pounce on the prey to be devoured, what matters is only waiting for the moment of the next surprise attack, and Aisha will never hesitate to seize what she thought of, whatever the cost.

On the other hand, the official (Salma) believed in the great actual difference between (Ibtisam) and her moody friend. It seemed to her that the kind young woman was psychologically stable compared to her friend, belonging to herself and the ideas she believed in, while her friend seemed to her as if she wanted everything from the world, and this is definitely impossible.

The simple party ended at five o'clock, and on the way back home, (Ibtisam) accompanied her friend (Aisha) in her car. The feelings of defeat were clearly visible on her face and on her eyebrows, so she looked weak and broken.

So she left herself to her friend (Ibtisam) to mention her perceptions of what happened at the bank party, and she kept watching the cars in silence.

It is most likely and certain that it is not easy for a person to arbitrarily believe that he is smarter than everyone, even if his thinking is like (Einstein) and the rest of his genius brothers.

Whereas, Mrs. (Salma) will not return the matter to the fact that (Aisha) does not have shame, but she is also bold to the point of recklessness, which directs her actions to absolute recklessness.

She also trusts herself in a somewhat extreme way, to the extent that it reaches the limits of selfishness and ingratitude, and it is wise for her at this age to wait for her destiny, not to seek to arrange her own destiny.

Because the issue here may be impossible, especially since we are all in a world of this complexity.

The days passed, her steps steady and accelerating, so Mrs. Salma took advantage of the matter in a way that made her imagine the events slowly and with deep thought and planning, so she argued that next Thursday is her birthday, and it is nice to see (Ibtisam) and her friend (Aisha) invited to a simple celebration that will be held in her house.

She also indicated that she would like (Ibtisam's) mother to come with her to participate, as she really wants to get to know her closely.

This was just an idea from a group of ideas that she started arranging with practices that do not cause any doubt. This lady wanted the waves of her thought to hit the shores of her thoughts successively, and the desired intent is to reveal the facts with a careful eye.

Doubt and Certainty

Mrs. Salma's birthday was the closest opportunity available to save the grieving mother from drowning in her grief since the death of the Father. Despite the stubbornness she showed at the beginning and her unwillingness to leave the house, Ibtisam's insistence on the matter contributed to the Mother's agreement to accept the invitation. If only as a way to go out for hours and escape from the clutches of that sad weather and its dominance through the hazy, dark thoughts.

It was seven o'clock in the evening when (Ibtisam) got into her car with her mother, and on the way she was stopped by her friend (Aisha) to take her with them to the house of Mrs. (Salma), and because of the dim modest street light, she did not notice the new suit that appeared on her and other matters of its own.

Without warning, (Ibtisam) decided to stop on the way in front of a flower shop, so she asked her mother's permission to bring some roses in a hurry.

As for the strange thing, her friend refused the idea of buying a bouquet of roses. Rather, it is strange that this sudden desire was not accepted by (Aisha), Where she found that it was a vulgar romance that was not appropriate for the birthday of their boss at work.

So she stopped the car in front of the flower shop, which is located right on the corner, and Ibtisam got out with her friend (Aisha), and they quickly entered the store with a smile radiating from Ibtisam's mouth.

They met a young man at their reception who was apparently calm and engaged in his work in arranging an exquisite multi-colored bouquet of roses. It also seemed clear that the mood of haste was and still is completely controlling Ibtisam's behavior at the time.

Despite the acceleration of the search in the store, Ibtisam saw a striking look of admiration from this young man, which means that she had touched something in his soul, which was that sudden feeling, and everything ended quickly. She gave him the price of a bouquet of roses, then she left in a hurry, but she did not even pay attention to his thanks. While her friend (Aisha) took another look at the young man, watching him from behind the glass, after (Ibtisam) left the store, she saw his volatile features.

On the road, the car was filled with silence as everyone was preoccupied with their concerns only. When (Ibtisam) arrived at Mrs. (Salma's) house, she searched for her white handbag, but she did not find it.

She was shocked because her whole life was in it, especially that paper on which she wrote her last thoughts, so she went crazy.

So she started searching, so who knows, perhaps it had fallen somewhere, but she did not find it, so (Aisha) referred to the young man who sold her roses, and he was the one who hid the bag!

And she confirms her words, claiming that she had noticed while she was taking a last look at the store that he was troubled, and in his looks there was apprehension, and fear radiated from his eyes.

As if he had committed a grave and unforgivable mistake, his eyes, with their experience, belong to the eyes of a professional thief, and they must return to the store immediately, with the help of the police, to avoid any reaction that may come from him.

Ibtisam's disorder prevented her from thinking properly, so perhaps the whole thing belonged to forgetfulness due to the excessive haste with which Ibtisam moved in and out of the store.

However, Aisha's constant pressure was due to the fact that the young man had contributed to Ibtisam's forgetting of her bag, so he had the idea of stealing it and putting it in a place where it was difficult to search with the lightness of the fingers of a professional magician.

The scene of the two girls entering the flower shop, accompanied by the policeman, was very shocking to the astonished young man. He did not understand until this moment where the problem was.

So he moved quickly and went in turn to the store manager to bring the girl's bag, expressing his great sadness that her phone was in the bag, so it was not easy for him to open it by force and then call his owner on the weakest possibilities.

Aisha's insistence was completely unnatural; her looks kept staring at his face with extreme precision, but she also began to check the movements of his body and confirmed with her intuition that the matter was not subject to chance at all but rather a demonic desire that invested her friend (Ibtisam) forgetting her bag with the intention of stealing it.

This was a strange insistence on her part, and the situation became embarrassing and difficult for his psyche, but he controlled his nerves, curbed his tongue, and stopped his tears.

Soon, the person in charge of the store intervened to push this offensive and disgraceful situation away from the silent young man, whose gaze did not leave the bouquets of roses stacked next to him.

The person in charge of the shop replayed the camera tape so that they could see with their own eyes how the young man received (Ibtisam) forgetting her white bag, and how he personally behaved after her quick exit from the place.

Replaying the videotape of the surveillance cameras was victorious for the smiling young man in order to see the justice of (God) in order to save his reputation. As for (Ibtisam), the situation was closer to a resounding fall into a deep well in which there is no decision.

She almost drowns out of her excessive sense of shame, as she was caught up in the story of the intended theft, which was just a spontaneous forgetfulness caused by haste.

The incident of losing the white handbag ended in peace and respect, despite the enormity of the situation for the calm young man, but from behind the glass of the shop he kept sighing as he looked at the tense young woman with a look that was not devoid of amazement but she was also mixed with silent admonition and some expressions of admiration revealed by his body movements when she spoke to him. Looks like when (Ibtisam) saw her, she almost pulled her heart out of her chest.

Thus, in anticipation of the lack of time, Ibtisam hurried to arrive again at the house of Mrs. (Salma), driving her small car and her heartbeat accelerating, beating with new tones that she was not familiar with before!

When Ibtisam arrived, she said: ("If Mrs. Salma asked us about the reason for the delay, we would say any reason other than what happened in the flower shop, for sure.")

On this evening, the picture was clearer, as the elegant young man (Hisham) appeared, the son of Mrs. (Salma), who noticed the warm welcome of his mother when she met Umm (Ibtisam); it seemed as if she knew her with great knowledge, but on the other side, it seemed that Um (Ibtisam) knew his aunt

(Khadija), who came late to participate in the evening, shortly after it had started, and the meeting between them was like a retelling of past memories.

It is clear that everyone at the party wears an ordinary dress, except for her friend (Aisha), who was under the influence of the lights, dressed remarkably, as if she had come on her wedding night and not just to participate in a birthday party with limited invitees.

It also smelled of a fragrant scent that reached the point of dominating the surrounding atmosphere.

The friend (Aisha) seemed to have signs of anxiety emanating from her looks, as there are signs of a new story being knit behind the scenes, as if she had transcended the meaning of weakness that ended her first night in the house of Mrs. (Salma).

And she came back again to practice reckless audacity and to look at (Hisham), and with her smile she tried to snatch conversations from him, even about personal matters that she did not know about his work and nature.

It seems that Mrs. Salma also had the intelligence that enabled her to give her son the opportunity to see the two models presented to him. He has the right to think carefully about the matter and decide of his own free will, without controlling his young thoughts.

Here is the brave young woman (Aisha) and here is the kind young woman (Ibtisam), who was not affiliated with the events of the evening as much as she belonged to what happened in the flower shop.

And most of all, these admiring looks, which appeared like a shining moon, are sincere from the eyes of this young man when (Ibtisam) came to the store.

It seems that at this moment something big may happen, or that the fates of love have chosen for her a big story whose chapters are beginning to be written on the pages of her life now.

Tomorrow, the conversation of the adults will release a grudge mixed with the magic of the past, while her intelligence gives her the transcendence and distance voluntarily from the open public communication between (Hisham) and her friend (Aisha).

Therefore, Ibtisam did not want to break into the dialogue, as her friend would not interpret the matter with good intentions but rather would accuse her of crowding her and obstructing her desires to finally get what she wanted.

Despite everything that indicates that the polite young man (Hisham) did not listen to what Aisha said and recounted, except that from time to time he sent glances from a distance that were a mixture of admiration for her friend (Ibtisam).

He had the desire to summon Ibtisam so that she would save him from Aisha's constant gossip about herself, her dreams, and her different thinking from the rest of the girls.

Time moved by the hands of the clock that indicated ten o'clock in the evening. Suddenly (Ibtisam) woke up from her dream to the sound of the call of Mrs. (Salma) and she called her son to be fair and distribute his speech between the two beautiful girls.

But even this polite joke did not get (Ibtisam) out of the control of the events of the flower shop, and what was in it from the looks of the young man who remained loyal to his first sight despite the tangle of events.

As for the flower shop, the young man was also wandering in his thoughts, as he did not want to mix his second look at her with any reproach that would hurt her feelings about this unjust accusation against him, which came to him at an unexpected fateful moment.

Immediately after that, he felt how beautiful feelings had crept into his heart by force at the sight of this girl, who did not come for a bouquet of roses as much as she came to change the course of his life.

In many cases, some hearts are struck by a lightning spark, in which the burning pain increases despite the attempts of their owners to extinguish their fire by adopting the principle of some intentional negligence.

But, unfortunately, they do not really have complete control over their unbridled feelings, which begin with rejection, and their smoke begins to rise, flying freely, so that love spreads between the ribs.

Returning to the circumstances of the Christmas party events, (Hisham) was not preoccupied with the somewhat silly conversation going on around him. It seems that he got involved in it with this young woman (Aisha), who in turn forgot everything completely, so that she did not interact with the rest of the invitees as if they were just human spectra moving around.

The repercussions of the incoherent conversation on everyone suggested distress, and that there was an exaggeration in this preoccupation that besieged her as she cast her net on the son of (Salma), and to be honest, the young man did not meet the ambition of any girl in the position of (Aisha) or (Ibtisam), as he looks somewhat handsome and graceful.

And he had his own activity through which he achieved his existence, and his mother, Mrs. Salma, who had nothing wrong with her.

Here (Ibtisam) moves silently and wanders around the hall. Sometimes she stands near the window looking at the sky and travels for a few moments to the stars, and sometimes she stands in front of the radio listening to the melodies of music playing with words. This is how she decided to live the moments without entering into conversations with adults or communicating in any way with (Hisham) and her friend, as scenes of the flower shop almost surround her.

For a girl or a woman in general, there are sensitive antennae that enable her in many cases to see this blazing peek of feelings, and her interpretation needs only to read the body language that is never wrong but rather scandalous.

It is the female's discernment, and perhaps this explains Aisha's mistrust of the young man and the deliberate accusation of theft against him.

It is certain that she had felt the extent of that passion, the flowing sensations that suddenly erupted from the eyes of this young man, who felt special feelings directed toward (Ibtisam) entirely, and (Ibtisam) did not try to go far in this thought, which means that reading the look had provoked the hatred of her friend, so she hastened to pounce and publicly defaming the young man.

Why does Ibtisam feel confused? Most likely, her friend will not leave her old way of thinking, as there is no look of admiration that she was exposed to throughout the years of friendship until Aisha was provoked by that.

Even if those words came from a mutual friend, and they did not come from a young man who was so well-groomed and handsome despite the fact that he was standing in a flower shop.

Which means that his condition as a whole may not be consistent with (Ibtisam's) circumstances if this view will develop into a situation greater than just ordinary admiration.

During this moment of joy, (Hisham) turns away and shows his indifference to the sticky conversations of her friend (Aisha).

And he went directly to this woman, sitting in a state that is closer to drowning in a sea of details that made her out of the evening.

She is not integrated in her mother's conversations with the acquaintances of the past, nor does she share their conversations with them, but she was in a state of complete isolation from the event, as if thus rejecting its existence.

Even Ibtisam was not consistent with sharing the conversation with others. What is happening in this girl's mind?

This is how (Hisham) was repeating it in secret, as he was attracted by a certain thing in her personality, and from afar, his mother (Salma) was following the event with caution on the one hand and trying to understand what made the young woman fall into this state of strange silence.

The young man (Hisham) approached her with strange boldness, and she argued to ask (Ibtisam) after he approached her: ("Why are you moving away with your imagination?") The pressure of the scene that preceded the birthday party was greater than trying to hide it, there she told him not to tell his mother about what happened before coming to the party. And in her voice was the roar of fears that the news would spread, and advice would be poured on her, and she would drown in it.

The strange thing is that she dared to tell him about the embarrassing situation in the flower shop and its developments, with which she felt pain and remorse.

It is not easy for her to accuse a good and trustworthy young man of stealing her bag, which she forgot due to negligence from being too hasty when she entered the shop.

She also hinted at how her friend (Aisha) was the one who insisted that the theft was an outright fabricated accident and not just an accidental forgetfulness.

(Hisham) feels surprised, apparently more than Ibtisam thinks, and he seemed to have a veiled anger infiltrating his facial expressions, so he took a quick look at (Aisha) in her place, and his features were not devoid of resentment, and when he asked her about the flower shop that she went to, she described the place without referring to his name, which was inadvertently omitted from the confusion of the situation, but she recognized the name of the street where he was.

The strange thing about this evening is that (Hisham) seemed to know this shop, but also the young man himself, so he quickly and in a low voice pronounces their conversation, saying:

It is (Azzam), and perhaps she remembered that the shop official called him to help him return the surveillance camera tape, so she said, smiling shyly: ("Yes… I think his name is (Azzam)".)

It was easy to understand the tender nature of the young woman (Ibtisam) at this moment. The situation hurt the pride of the young man, who gave logical justifications that prevented him from contacting the owner of the bag. Indeed, he would not be able to open her phone and then call to ask her to receive her bag, and he was at the top of sophistication and morals. She immediately remembered the attitudes of her absent father.

In another corner close to the scene, Mrs. Salma's face seemed to indicate satisfaction that her son had finally spoken to the young woman (Ibtisam), while on the other side, her mother was also able here to understand what Mrs. Salma was aiming for behind organizing this celebration of her birthday. And what was the intent of that, and with all transparency, she was smiling as she followed the course of events despite her preoccupation with her sister (Khadija).

On the other hand, the features of defeat were visible on the face of the brave young woman (Aisha), who, through her long conversation with (Hisham), could not extract that interest from him for a few minutes, equivalent to his quick conversation with her friend (Ibtisam).

This new situation meant that some confusion would occur to Aisha until the evening ended.

What made matters more complicated and increased the pace of her heartbreak that kills dreams was Hisham's keenness to take Ibtisam's phone number without asking her for the same request.

The shock of the judge paralyzed her tongue, so she watched everyone in silence, her features laconic and calm, until the end of the party.

How can I ignore those charming smiles? I can't control my feelings when he looks at me... I lose my sanity!

Anxiety

On the way back home, time stops in the mind of (Ibtisam), who seemed to be wandering with her imagination, and after the arrival of her friend (Aisha), she did not focus on what was going on around her; even her mother (Fatima) was also swimming in the streams of successive events in silence.

As for the quiet young woman, Ibtisam, she bet that she would not find sleep at the first attempt but rather she would feel remorse until she found a successful way to express her apology to the young man for her annoying reaction.

On that lunar night, her bed became like a rug of thorns, and the pain could not be broken except by returning to the looks of that young man whom fate had suddenly cast in her face to possess her heart.

He immediately gave her indications that in this life there are other beautiful feelings that should be directed to a young man who might be suitable to enter the orchards of her life and settle down.

She wondered why she lived in this way of emotional stagnation. Did she, like her father, have a central personality who could only live for herself? But she was never this model who could win for himself in the absolute.

She only saw life from her own personal angle, and she does not remember many details of her first adolescence and its events.

Her father's strictness toward her and her sister was to make her achieve his dreams, through which he wanted to imbue them with masculine qualities in order for her to face life with firmness befitting this difficult time.

Therefore, the spectrum of the man she desired did not visit her dreams, and his image was not formed in a spectrum that might make her define her ambitions in the man of her future, so for her, it was like a mirage that was not worth pursuing at all.

With the merciful heart of a mother, the sad lady realized that her daughter was suffering from something, and she did not translate what she saw of (Hisham) at the end of the evening with her daughter (Ibtisam).

She was wandering in another world, as if she had come to the evening against her will. She invested in what she felt that her daughter could not easily find sleep, and she entered the room to ask her what disturbed her peace during the celebration of the birthday of Mrs. Salma, who insisted on her presence in order to celebrate with her with love.

So, she started answering her questions with confidence, and the sadness in her voice was evident. Was it necessary for the police to come, or was it appropriate for them not to come at all?

But the first look of admiration apparently provoked (Aisha's) feelings, so she was eager to spoil this conversation that had just begun between Ibtisam's eyes and the looks of the young seller.

This is how she began to explain to her mother the circumstances of the accident after she returned to the house, where she told her the full details of it. Therefore, she was all the time looking for an ideal solution to wash away the clutches of her act that caused the young man to be broken, when she ran after miserable thoughts that her friend (Aisha) made; that put her in this difficult circumstance, and she pays for it through remorse.

This explains her daughter's departure from the evening and the lack of interest in the presence of (Hisham), the son of her boss, who seemed to her to be a remarkable young man. It was necessary for her to get to know him more than the image that happened when she left him for (Aisha).

Where Aisha practiced on him a case that is closer to hunting, although it was a naïve desire and he was not in his form fit for this desire in the first place.

In parts of the hidden night, and time runs parallel to the thoughts, and it is about to reach its middle, as the time races to announce that the clock has reached twelve exactly, there is another night in which the party did not end with Mrs. (Salma).

After Mrs. Salma's insistence, her son (Hisham) obeys her to tell her the real reason that made (Ibtisam) look so sad, then he asked her for a promise to keep this matter a secret so that his image would not be shaken in front of her, as he promised her not to reveal it to anyone.

And until he finished the motherly conversation, while she was waiting to hear what indicates that he had admired (Ibtisam), he told her that the admiration had occurred, even if her friend from another angle had touched something in himself despite her worrisome audacity.

He also continued his conversation with her to tell her his actual feelings, as he loves those kind of brave girls who prefer attacking to defense without indifference.

But at the same time, he did not hide his concern about her after he heard the story of the flower shop from her friend (Ibtisam), as this type of people make him repel.

Back at Ibtisam's house, the lunar night ended with all its minute details with her mother, and early in the morning, before going to the bank, she decided to pass her cars to the flower shop, perhaps she would really be able to find a state of apology with refined feelings that befitted what she had expressed last night.

Unfortunately, she found the store closed, so she waited for a while, turned around, picked up a phone number, wrote it down immediately, and then moved on.

At the bank, things were more complicated for Mrs. (Salma). She did not want to tell (Ibtisam) what she learned from her son, but she told her that the coming days are the last days of her friend (Aisha) in the bank, so she will try hard to transfer her to one of the branches that needs her experience. So Ibtisam thought that the coming days would not be in her favor, nor in the interest of her friend either.

Most of what was preoccupying (Ibtisam) was her fear of (Aisha's) reactions and her mistrust in interpreting such a move with incalculable results. Perhaps she was obsessed with the fact that she was the one who prompted the manager (Salma) to take a decision to transfer her from the main branch.

But from the consequences of what happened to her in the flower shop, from this moment on, she no longer cares about her friend's explanations. All the justifications that Aisha gives are always subject to bad faith.

When the name (Hisham) appeared on her phone screen, (Ibtisam) was confused and her cheeks turned red immediately, so she tried as much as she could to adjust her features in front of Mrs. (Salma).

It seems that he has invested his knowledge in the young flower seller, and he wants her to go with him so that he can do for her what comforts her, and nothing will comfort her except a proper apology and a request to forgive her for what happened.

Indeed, the content of the communication was heading toward fulfilling this urgent desire, so Ibtisam wanted to speak the truth. Therefore, she told Mrs. Salma, over the phone, her humanitarian position.

So she, in turn, blessed this good moral behavior, once for her apology to the young man and another time for her son (Hisham) to find the perfect opportunity to see from (Ibtisam) what is greater than yesterday's talk.

(Ibtisam) left her car in the bank's yard and rode with (Hisham), who seemed to know the store for sure, so they stopped in front of the entrance and entered the store. She did not turn forward but found it wise to walk in the back.

She does not know the secret of that. Is it the shyness that afflicted her at these moments? Or does she want to be sure that his new look may differ from his looks yesterday because she wants to make sure of something? (Hisham) quickly said: "Hello (Azzam)."

As soon as Azzam turned to him and (Ibtisam) appeared next to Hisham, there was no sign on (Azzam's) face that he was sad. Rather, he produced again the same sympathetic glance, and perhaps something greater than it.

She could not explain this longing, as Azzam appeared as if he really, without any doubt, was waiting for her presence, and she felt his anguish through his looks.

He knew instinctively that a girl of this degree of delicacy and humanity would not let things go in vain, scattered in the void, and would come to him in order to apologize and extract forgiveness from him.

Accusing him of theft by force is an attack on her humanity before his humanity, and those who are in her delicacy can never continue to practice arrogance over people's feelings.

As for the strange thing, (Hisham) possessed the intelligence that enabled him to reinterpret the scene realistically. These exchanged looks from the eyes of (Ibtisam) or the eyes of (Azzam) wanted to say something bigger and deeper than even the idea of an apology, despite the availability of its reasons.

But he did not comment and let her words wash away what happened and let Azzam experience the impact that his admiring glances had on her, which shot like lightning as soon as he saw her at the entrance of his place.

Love is a song

The words of phrases of apology and gestures of forgiveness are over, and there are no more desires and wishes that those wandering eyes say, and the eyes are no longer able to control their language.

Perhaps (Hisham) should have left immediately, leaving, inspired by his experience, indicating that a beautiful love story is about to start writing its chapters with their hands together on the pages of their next lives.

But he could not leave her, as she must return to the bank again, as her work day is not over yet, and before leaving, Azzam saluted them, so he heard from (Hisham) that he wanted to sit with him as he was missing him.

But what was a remarkable sign was the palm of (Ibtisam), who sank in the palm of (Azzam) for a while, clearly declaring that the story had other dimensions, so he gave her his personal card containing his phone numbers.

The tender young woman did not believe that love happened from a mere glance that crossed the limits of feelings to settle in the heart and that the impressions of the fleeting meeting continued to haunt her, not budging from her thoughts.

It is possible that the stereotypical image of the youth of these days, which made her fall into the clutches of admiration for him, may differ, but the puzzling question remains, (did he really feel that she was attracted to him?)

And the days went by without her realizing it, and the dates fell from her agenda, so she dared and finally called him so that he would write down her own number. Waiting for her was difficult and abhorrent throughout the successive days when his name did not appear on her phone screen.

Perhaps he was not interested in contacting and asking about her, and he certainly did not feel anything about her, which he considered a mere phantom, but it was imperative that he at least talk to her; to feel a hypothetical difference between his voice in nature and his voice over the phone.

But she wondered: What are these assumptions that lead her to the shores of confusion? When she reached this conclusion, she kept laughing while thinking in a way that was not devoid of teenage feelings. What different voice is she talking about?

But she could not get rid of this terrible grief that erupted from his voice, which sounded sad and defeated in an unequal battle. She did not know why she called him again, as she was trying to break the silence, so perhaps there is something in his world that would prevent him from doing so?

And this is how she was all day, even when she was lying on her pink bed looking for the answers that escaped from her. Who knows, she might find these answers, then she suddenly stops and continues to sail in the sea of her thoughts while looking at the white ceiling of her room in silence.

And every ringing of the phone became a reflection of a state of overwhelming longing; she seemed tense as soon as she sat at her desk in her place at the bank, and some seemed surprised about the way she handles her phone at every ringing, especially Mrs. (Salma).

She rushes immediately and aggressively, dragging him to stick it to her ears and saying in a loud, audible voice: "(Hello) and on the other side, the caller is not the sweetheart she is waiting for".

This chaotic feeling has become painful and budges her delicacy when the sound is far from the sound she loves to hear.

And the most painful thing for her is that curiosity in the looks of others, in which many questions appear that they would like to ask in a direct way: "(Who are you waiting for to contact you?)".

In fact, that young woman did not need this state of love, as she trusted in her beauty, femininity, and tender beauty. She just wanted to employ her talents to obtain a positive feeling that could be directed to a man she thought deserved all of her overwhelming sympathy.

When this model invaded her life, Ibtisam did not want to give in to the feeling of a girl who needed a hug haunted by fatherhood to throw herself into his arms.

What was hidden was greater than her concern alone, as the situation is no different for the young man (Azzam), as she is a duplicate identical to her burning feelings, and his feelings are no different from the feelings of that young girl who took over his being and sat on the throne of his heart.

The hour of his life halts the events and stands still, as if time had stopped at her looks.

He, too, kept looking from a hidden side at his new life, and apprehension became the companion of his nights, and questions came to his mind. Is this the love he hears about in stories?

But the luxury of love in the reality of life will not allow him to impersonate a strong passion toward a girl. It seems from the details of her conversations that she belongs to a social level that exceeds his capabilities in all realism, where the dream will always remain just a mirage that he can never possess.

He went back to doing his daily work, immersing himself in his work, which he had mastered, with his fingers planting plants in pots. It may have been a miserable attempt on his part to forget the pain of thinking of smiling.

Despite his alleged preoccupation, he kept falling into the trap of looking at his phone. At least, there is hope in him that informs him that it exists, even as a name present in his life.

He apparently wanted to impersonate courage with her, to practice daring with all his heroic classes, but whenever he looked at his phone screen, he always failed to press the call button; until he hears her voice swimming in sweetness.

Her voice has a sweetness that touches his feelings and moves the bells of his heart, so she bridles his tongue so that she can win by narrating what she wants.

Those sentences were filled with poetry with feminine words that imposed their tyranny on his thoughts, so she followed them.

While (Ibtisam) lives while waiting for him, it is a one-sided match of patience; she does not know who will design it or how it will end will he be the initiator first or she?

It is waiting with a unique taste, sometimes with a bitter taste, and at other times, it is a wait that is more delicious than honey. Here she is eagerly accepting her phone, holding it with her fingers, moving it and shaking it, then feeling his screen, hoping that he will feel her flowing affection to tell him about it. Obviously, life swallowed him up with its preoccupations.

She is imprisoned between the bars of her shyness, wishing the soul a connection that does not reflect anything greater than his human sense of it.

And why does she not say openly that she fell in love with him to the point of recklessness, and it hurts her that he did not try to contact her, and on the other hand, she does not want to ask Hisham about him either.

Here she is, finally, standing behind the glass of the flower shop, glimpsing him with her looks. She left thinking aside and overcame her pride, and started calling him. He did not notice at first, but he crossed over to her, bypassing the bouquets of roses.

He sent a smile of gratitude and contentment far away, and she replied with the same and better one, but he did not have the courage to give her what indicated that he had actually fallen in love with her.

The fog of silence spread again in her life, but she went away and became isolated from her family surroundings, just as she was isolated from the work environment, with which she lived a full life in her imagination.

(Azzam) had the experience to make him realize what is her feelings that began to crystallize toward him, and he bets on the impossibility of things developing beyond a passing fateful encounter that has nothing to do with its events.

Thus, his traces will end and the winds of days will quickly wipe him away. He used to talk to himself as he flipped some lotus flowers. Then he asked in a whisper while speaking to those roses scattered around him:

(Why doesn't she look carefully at that struggle that I live with all its events? My credibility and honor will not accept that I break into her life in these circumstances from which she only knows my happy smiles, which are renewed sorrows for me.)

Through his straying into the unknown, he was crying for himself, and the only honest logic was for him to embrace her until he perished, so he would not avoid looks that gave him the confidence that was absent from him and that he was still able to persuade a girl of that level of goodness who was striving to meet him and look at him in order to transmit special feelings to him.

(Ibtisam) also remained absent-minded, peeping, swearing in secret that she could hear his groaning, and wanted to shout at him: *(Get rid of these obsessions.)*

She almost did what he was thinking of, getting up, embracing him, and crying, not knowing, despite this amount of grief, why she felt a moral responsibility moving within her to protect him from the agonizing grief over him?

Doubt is cut off by certainty, and the sun is never obscured by a sieve. (Ibtisam) fell in love with the young man (Azzam), and he, in turn, reached with her an extreme passion that must crystallize for something, or a love story with clear features that has no alternative.

This is the truth in its abstract form as it passes, so it was necessary for things to evolve between them, but who can remove this ambiguity from its path and from his path in the same way?

If she goes to (Hisham) directly to find out from him who this mysterious young man is, perhaps he will move toward her heart with the looks of infatuation, and she is afraid that his involvement in her world will shock him and he may stir special feelings toward her, but he is of the intelligence that will definitely help him in extrapolating the matter clearly.

On the other hand, there was nothing greater than an initial acquaintance that did not reach the threshold of a state that may be described as admiration that could develop into a great love story.

This young man (Hisham) was up to her expectations. The manner of his reception of her in one of the downtown shops had changed, and at her request, she was no longer a girl likely to enter his life as much as she became for him just a close friend, and she is always accompanied by great recommendations from his mom to take care of her because she sure is a different girl.

On the other hand, he was not that young man of fragile intelligence, as he realized that the meeting, in a large part of his moments, aimed to talk about (Azzam) in one way or another.

Perhaps without getting involved in any introductions, he deliberately forgot that she existed, so he started talking about him, recounting the story of his life. His father was a close friend of his father, who cared for him for a while before he died.

Man was created free, but in this worldly life there are obstacles and ceilings that force him to stay in his place, standing, awaiting him in front of this innate freedom and its details.

It does not destroy him, but it does send subtle messages that his perceptions of the absolute and the complete are not always accurate.

You always remain the son of circumstances, drinking from their events, and you do not have the choice, but no matter how miserable factors surround you sometimes, it is not wise to frustrate you and hinder you.

And it is certain that some hopes that realistic perceptions stop will take him, as this girl belongs to a rich family, and she can reduce the path of ambitions with proactive steps, she is remarkably rich beyond imagination, and she possesses many magic keys.

She secretly wishes to meet someone who belongs to her community, knows exactly what his goal is, and even has a social network that generously produces opportunities to seize one of them.

However, despite these realistic hypotheses, the winds are blowing in a way that ships do not desire. With the crushing feeling of poverty, responsibilities become inflated and wishes escape, leaving them imprisoned in the papers of stories.

For a person to feel that there is a whole world hanging around his neck, waiting for the fruit of his quest in life in order to share it with him and take from the balance of his enjoyment of the joys of life.

Here the chariot of life gets heavier and the gears get stuck, so that the feeling of poverty becomes an ordeal every day, in which the need for bread increases before getting new shoes, and the questions become unanswered on the ground but are brought by fate.

The wait is long until the hour of the end comes for a new generation to begin carrying the banner of poverty and its weapon of ignorance.

Even you, who are reading my story or standing behind the walls of the city following its events; In fact, you may possess an acceptable level of talent.

But this obedient master called poverty sometimes kills your talents before they are born or incites them in his relentless quest to crystallize into a meaning greater than them and to become criminal, in which hatred for society is embodied, and it becomes an inevitable monetary feature, and rarely what happens that impedes the conditions of poverty and getting out of its barren orchards.

This is how (Azzam) was telling himself at the inevitable hour of confession, as he did not wish that his father would die in his hands, nor that he would breathe his last, until his father puts him with his death on the real, actual test.

He views his education as a luxury that cannot be sustained and even takes care of an entire family under the pressure of circumstances that will never pity him.

Likewise, he watched the image of his orphaned sister besieging him, her black and faded images from everywhere, chanting the lost tenderness and the dignified life stolen by the death of her father, and despite the passage of all these years, he still heard the cries of empty stomachs that played the melody of the pain of hunger.

This was what destroyed every beautiful human feeling, but what does he do? How does he complete his family's journey, and where does he start? The answers, as usual, are definitely missing!

This abstract meaning was evident as soon as he returned from his father's funeral, as the school appeared to him as a terrifying spectrum.

His mother and sister look at him, inviting him to exert effort and hard work since from that moment, he became responsible for them, and for him it was a decisive and unfair moment in his life, for which he paid dearly.

The distressed (Azzam) thought that he was not alone, as he had a family that embraced him according to kinship. The uncles' system moved in a frantic competition compared to the role of the intrusive uncles, who have nothing to help the widowed mother and her two sons.

As for the catastrophe that fate will bring, it may lie in his uncles, who will with extreme precision pave a road of ideas that contribute to saving the family of their deceased brother and may be implemented with limitless violence and cruelty.

All the senior men of the family agreed, with a clear and convincing human will, to marry the afflicted widow to one of his uncles.

Naturally, the reason was ready at the time, which is that the uncle, according to social norms, is necessary for him to play this moral role after the death of his brother and to take care of his grieving family with his death.

And to be honest, without (Azzam) openly slandering the hidden intentions of his uncles, this is conclusive evidence of humiliation and baseness of morals. These were never the intended or alleged reasons.

Behind this perception was a system of intrigue and envy that wanted in any way to control the legacy of the deceased brother and harm it in the easiest way, even if the share was only for a single widow woman with her two weak children.

His father was a half-brother; his mother died young; he married another woman, the mother of his great uncles; and when his father died, he did not earn anything from his money, as it was his aunt, his father's wife, who took over the family's affairs.

And he tasted a lot of ill-treatment from it, so he was destitute and could hardly have his daily sustenance, while the uncles got the fruits of his grandfather's struggle.

And on the opposite side of the life of family misery was his mother (Saeeda), despite all the signs of extreme poverty spread throughout the house, fiercely fighting the siege imposed on her before and after her husband's death.

Her beauty, striking the gaze of men, caused hardships for her husband. His brothers envied him for being the poor man who married a woman of such beauty.

The matter is clear and does not need proofs. They don't seek her help out of pure affection for their nephews.

In the matter, there is a desire greater than the concept of assistance, which resides within it a hidden bad intention.

They are pushing her fiercely to marry the uncle of her children as soon as she finishes her waiting months without delay, while they could have helped her without implicating her in an inevitably fatal test with such cruelty.

At an important juncture in the life of (Azzam), he did not realize the reasons for the intransigence with which his desperate mother confronted this desire. He did not know, given his young age, what to say or how to act toward this secret of rejection!

This uncle was not so bad in manners, which gives her the categorical and angry right to reject him completely when she heard indications of his desire to implement his aims and not to take into account the circumstances in which she lives.

He does not know if the refusal was in fulfillment of the memory of his late father? Or is she unwilling to respond to his hasty-step request, and with great stubbornness he desires to implement it? She rejects the logic inherent in the idea of being helped by his generous uncles.

It is certain that she hates them all, as she always thinks about where they were when their poor brother was suffering greatly in order to feed her with her two sons.

The justified giving has no moral value. Giving throughout the ages remains the giving without an expected return. If it is linked to a desired human purpose or goal, it no longer has any return that triumphs for one's humanity.

Rather, its value disappears, and it turns immediately into a worldly personal interest, and in it the profit fights fiercely, and it will not be satisfied with the loss.

This mother, despite the control of poverty in all the details of her life's destiny, did not seem to lose her victory over the true meaning of a life of dignity, and this family, despite its relative superiority over his father in terms of wealth.

She could not convince his mother, or perhaps she did not want to hurt her two children, and in the heart of her calculations was the dear son (Azzam), but this disturbing question was the one that really strained her psyche.

So why does the widowed mother not sacrifice for their sake and accept an actual reality with what her present share has written for her and what awaits her in the prosperous future when she is still young and wanted?

And with some interest in herself and an investment in the wealth of the uncle who wants to marry her, she may return to her true self as a truly beautiful lady who blooms like a white lily.

For him, he wonders where his mother came from with all this courage and bravery in her valiant resistance against the mighty uncle and repelling his continuous and brutal attack without mercy expected from him.

And she endured the hardships and fought epics at the peak of heroism while she spoke to his uncle with such recklessness and indifference, declaring its complete rejection of the entire idea and will bear the consequences of this outright stubbornness.

The issue within the framework of the social environment in which they live almost reaches the rank of prevailing custom and observed matters.

There, Azzam realized that the day that ended was not the same as the days to come, so when he brought up the idea of him leaving school, her silence most likely supported the desire.

So she went to a corner inside her room and did not comment, so the poor boy left the school, almost seeing the difficulty of the coming days embodied before his weeping eyes.

The boy (Azzam) moved at that time to the place of an old man located near their residence, in whom he saw the ideal father who did not abandon him, but he did not sympathize with him enough.

His daily salary barely sufficed for bread and some food, not to mention the harassment of customers, the free looks of sympathy that did not go beyond mere sorrow, and some stupid insinuations from some women who had heard about his uncle's desire to marry his beautiful mother.

One day, while he was walking on the road, one of his teachers called him to ask him about the secret of his absence and why he stopped attending school. He told him that his father had died, and tears were falling from his eyes, and that it was no longer a luxury for him to continue his studies.

The family needs him to sacrifice and go to a job that may help his mother, in addition to his father's modest pension, so that life can continue.

For him, the worst experience for himself was his leaving school, as one of its negative results was that his talent for drawing and shaping clay was disrupted, in a very important sign of the presence of an artist hiding within his restless soul. And who is eager at this time to realize obtaining enough money to continue the life of the mother and sister.

With the passage of time and years, her feelings about his life fluctuated. He thought carefully, and after the catastrophic failure of his first work experiences, he decided to move to live and work in one of the industrial cities, which are located on the outskirts of the city.

He is satisfied with his only role, which is only to send financial support to his mother in order to also save the value of meals that he may have to eat at home.

He went out carrying his dreams on his shoulder and carrying in his hand the bag of his old worries, and he did not pay any attention to the idea of being with his mother and sister, because money is the most urgent priority in such circumstances, so that he only spoke to his mother with a few sentences that proved his good choice.

And when he left his house, he went out without saying hello to her or his sister, so did he announce his public escape by doing so?

But in the bitter reality of the matter, the society of the industrial city, to which he was led by the movement of his destinies, did not provide him with the desired morsel, not even enough sustenance to continue the struggle and be patient with the difficulty of life away from his mother and sister, as well as the neighborhood in which he grew up; where are the places of old play and the amputated happiness that was assassinated by early orphan hood?

One day, (Azzam) suffered from a health problem that forced him to stay in bed and did not go out to work. It was a good coincidence that he was visited from time to time by a young man from his colleagues, not much older than him, called (Imran).

The strange thing is that he was similar to him in many details of his life, and whoever watches them thinks that they are two brothers or twins who have been brought up by life with its ups and downs, so they shared their circumstances drawn on the pages of destinies together.

Everyone felt the extent of the spiritual closeness between these two young men, and there was a strong relationship between them that was free of suspicion. They came to work together and went out together, even in the restaurant, sitting close to each other.

As for what is funny, they eat from the same plate in the sense that they share a loaf of bread, and smiles radiate on their faces, clearly consolidating the true meaning of friendship.

This new friend is also an orphan, but he left his home after a massive revolution that swept his being and overturned the scales of his usual sobriety witnessed by the impact of his mother's sudden, quick marriage after the death of his father in a horrific and frightening traffic accident.

He was unable to complete his education due to the extreme hardship he was subjected to with his mother's new husband and the strange details of his mother's complete submission to his will.

And in the hours of serenity on the river of loneliness, Imran goes on speaking smoothly and tells Azzam about his secrets, as if he is letting himself go about her pains that have nested between his ribs for years, and his soul refuses to leave the branches like crows standing tall and crowing in a soul-destroying voice.

To tell him, with bitterness that filled his voice with some pain, that his father was absent and traveling a lot, and his mother used to stay alone with him in their apartment, and the only companion they had in this abandonment was the sound of the television.

He mentions in his pure hadiths that he repeatedly tried to complete his education using legitimate means; he complains to his relatives, but they are no different from his deceitful stepfather, so tomorrow reality throws him into a rocky cave that shatters his ambitions.

Even in small matters, he is haunted by complete failure, so people's comments pounce on him and tear his feelings apart.

As usual, his stepfather shows his fangs mockingly, spewing his poison to destroy his dreams with his words.

The presence of the inquisitive and unjust husband of the young man (Imran) marked the end of his life with his mother, so he was suffocating his freedom with the gallows of customs, calling him the worst descriptions and belittling him in front of everyone, and in front of his mother, he mastered his harm, and she adopted silence as a refuge for her, or perhaps as if she agreed to exercise his absolute power over the life of her only son.

Fate wanted to give the two young men a small ray of lost hope in obtaining a decent life together like the rest of human beings. The return may not exceed a few dirhams, but it will be sufficient to sow joy in their thirsty souls to achieve confidence in the aspirations of their life path, so will the future be different from its present brother?

It seems that (Imran) was affected by the circumstances of his owner (Azzam), and he kept visiting him during his illness, sitting with him in his small room, which barely accommodates one bed and one wooden chair and resembles a prison, intending to check on his health.

He would bring him food in addition to treatment and sometimes help him get up and take him to the bathroom if necessary, without shame.

And he did so with a broad smile, full of glee.

The equality of people in their tragedies gives them, in many cases, a strong human bond for their relationship with each other.

When grief spreads and the abyss of grief widens, hearts usually unite.

The true comprehensive meaning of these united hearts is formulated in dream and torment, so perhaps salvation will happen and aspirations will be fulfilled, so distress will be relieved and worries will melt.

Azzam's work was not merciful in its infancy. In these industrial cities, a person appears as a small cog in a huge machine that drives profit at any cost.

It is run from the fuel of the people of need and destitution who left their world that they know for the sake of another new world that may actually be greater than their imaginations, and Azzam was a young boy; manhood was forced upon him, and he forcibly accepted it.

The young man was unable to resist the life of the industrial cities, and then he was repeatedly trying to adapt in a crazy way.

And he tries to impersonate patience; perhaps he came out of the experience with a profession that might enable him – when he was able to develop it – to join another place, and with other conditions that would bring him dignity before abundant money.

But no way, dreams do not build a tangible reality as much as they build palaces above the clouds. The factory owners, under the pressure of high raw materials, were forced to lay off him and dozens of workers, including (Imran) as well.

And here is life being harsh on him again, as if it hates him to the exclusion of humans.

These sentences were coming out of his mouth while he was talking to his friend (Azzam), and some tears were falling as he was trying to catch them with his dirty hands.

And because every darkness can be broken through by a small star of optimism passing through the sky of life, one of their old colleagues sympathized with them and mediated for them to work in another place in another city in an iron and steel factory.

They had an answer with a recommendation sent to someone who might have mercy in his heart and refuse the profit equation.

The two young boys arrived in the new city, and optimism radiated from their eyes and enthusiasm appeared in their weak and skinny bodies. The facilities of the new city seemed, with the first impression, another picture of the suffering of the former industrial city.

It is no different from it; the confusing crowds fill its roads, the expatriates live in its buildings, and the salaries are almost enough to cover life with a little.

(Imran) was trying to comfort his owner's miserable condition with his remarkable wit, so he would tell jokes with his brown face and move his eyebrows, and he would deliver sentences and say his comments sarcastically on a laughing scene passing in front of them, as he is a clown, or, in a more accurate sense, an actor who is skilled in imitation.

He imitated in front of him the manner of speaking of their manager in the old, fat factory, so he walked slowly and dragged his legs while breathing hard, placing his hand on his stomach, and uttering an incomprehensible roar.

But laughter was far from (Azzam's) features, as there was not a fleeting moment of absent-mindedness without remembering school, missing company, and above all, painting and sculpture, the two hobbies that were interrupted.

He almost no longer holds a pen, and finds the spirit that enables him to draw, and he does not find a single piece of wood in which he can engrave something or create any aesthetic formation that satisfies him.

In a visit dominated by the mood of haste, (Azzam) visited his mother and sister and gave her an envelope with trembling hands, so his mother took out what was in it, and when she found him carrying a little help, she did not control her face, which gave him a painful feeling of resentment.

Her features announced that his pursuit of life would not lead to anything. His desire was to spend the night at home, but the sight of his mother (Saeeda) receiving him did not give him a chance to spend a day or two at the very least.

So he left at sunset, returning to the city in which he works, so what is wrong with his mother, who has lost the language of communication and encouragement that helps him to face his failure and his successive defeats, as long as he works in that way from weak revenues, and he has nothing to do about this living life that does not want to change as if it is proceeding monotonously in the same place.

The sad boy went to work with another man, who seemed to him to be more merciful compared to the worker who left for a short vacation and did not return, so (Azzam) loved learning from this sympathetic, kind, and decent worker, and his enthusiasm increased.

And if the fruit of labor here will not bring enough money at worst, nothing less than learning a new distinguished profession, which may benefit him later if he moves to another city.

What Hisham did not know about Azzam's life at this stage was that he did not encounter tangible luxury from anyone in that forgotten part of the world, so he kept drawing without feeling any clear trace of what he was making.

It was a sign of a murderous emptiness, or he was an insignificant young man who had time to fiddle with his quill on the walls; to perpetuate the memory of his passage to this place.

But when the owner of the factory happened to pass one morning and asked who had made these figures on the walls, he might have mixed a sense of admiration with a feeling of resentment at such actions.

So when he converted to the young man (Azzam), he kept swearing by (God) with the firmest faith that the drawing takes place away from working hours.

The man was smiling while he was only expressing his admiration, so the poor young man dared and told him about the small sculptures that he fashioned from the stones of the region, but receiving art in itself is a talent no less than the talent of those who practice it, but the financial man did not like what he saw, despite his falling into the circle of admiration for him aptly.

But he advised him to focus on work and strive to overcome the characteristics of a simple worker. To rise to the status of a skilled worker who can stand to work alone without much help from anyone.

Therefore, for subsequent years, (Azzam) was not interested in their number; he continued to work and save, despite the pressures of life; he kept depriving himself of various pleasures to save, and he could send any financial support to his mother and sister.

And at a defining moment of his estrangement in pursuit of livelihood, he decided to leave the factory and return to the heart of the city, and for the first time since his return he thinks positively, liberating his talent from the power of lost dreams.

The matter requires that he strive to realize an idea from outside the box. For the length of his stay in the industrial cities, he did not know his bets on the coming days, especially considering the reliance on his talent.

So does he practice painting or sculpture without studying or school education through which he develops these talents? It was certainly not possible for him to practice them within the framework of an organized study. He will need additional years, and new obstacles will arise for him that he is indispensable at the present time, and the situation will lead to more out of misery.

While (Azzam) was walking in one of the town's markets, he happened to see one of his teachers in the old school that he had abandoned against his will. The teacher's features seemed sad, as he learned the real reasons when he asked about him.

And when he told him that he was looking for an activity in line with his talent in drawing and sculpting and that he had a little money that might help him start with a modest first step, it was important for him to start, there he advised him to do something that people flocked to.

And he must go to one of the huge commercial centers and explore the matter with his own eyes; perhaps he will find something that he can do, and who knows, his talent will have the decisive factor in accessing the corridors of money from where he does not know at all, as he advised him to wait before starting any work that he will perform.

Thinking must take its time until a person reaches results that fulfill his wishes in reality, not on the wishes of dreams.

At first, he thought that his teacher was advising him in anticipation of a day when he would rent a place, but the man seemed to understand the concerns of his truly talented student when he told him of his desire for an activity that he could practice even in one of the rooms of the house.

Then the activity expands if it encounters success that satisfies it and satisfies its long-repressed ambitions.

The talented young man arrived at one of the centers and in a hurry started wandering among its wide corners, looking closely at the shops. He wants to catch an infernal idea that will fulfill his ambitions. He goes up to one floor and goes down to another.

The gift corner caught his attention, and he found that the artistic direction was very poor and expensive, as there were no dazzling aesthetics that justified the high price of gift boxes as well as other accessories.

Soon he kept in his memory some of the necessary details that he saw from here and there; his eyes were like a camera taking pictures, and when he returned home, he began designing the first box inspired by his imagination. When he finished showing it to whomever he trusted in his taste, he found that it had convinced him.

He returned again to add more shapes to it based on the central shape, which gave it an additional beauty that attracts the eyes of the onlookers.

The market movement was not wide enough to give him a sense of profit, so he tried to pass by one of the gift shops in another large shopping center to offer him his products, and he finally had what he wanted.

The owner of the shop was amazed and impressed, which seemed to be noticeable on his face, so he took him inside to conclude a business deal with him.

At first, he asked to give him enough money so that he could create various new forms with different specifications and to give him a profit that exceeds what the talented young artist aims for.

But for the sake of this goal, he stipulated that he should continue to work for him exclusively, for everything that his talent is capable of; it is the private property of this shop and its owner only.

Only two months had passed, complete days, and (Azzam) had breathed absolute freedom without restrictions, with expanding lungs for the first time.

And here he is touching with his hand prosperity that he had not experienced before in the entire course of his previous life, making sure that this money belongs to him and not to anyone else.

He put it on the table where he works, plans, draws, and paints, then he begins to smile – a smile of joy, not a smile of sadness.

It seems to him that sadness has a joy that can only be felt by those who have lived in the crucible of pain.

His self-confidence, along with his belief in his talent, may have the means that, after a terrible long wait, gave him the ability to overcome a comprehensive state of need, and here he is, in the last line of his tragedy poem, reaching the sufficient profit to achieve what he wishes.

But when talking about the flower shop in which he works, his standing there was nothing but an attempt by him to return the favor to the man who gave him the place and the money to create his works.

Perhaps I love him with an exceptional love!
He is still silent, not reciprocating my feelings. Does he love me?

The Sun of Longing

Hisham's talk about Azzam was rich in minute details, telling the shocked young woman his life story as if it were a fantasy.

Is it possible for people to live among us with this much suffering and misery?

And what are these destinies that shape our lives and chart for us paths without mercy, devoid of pity, with all power.

The features of the young woman (Ibtisam) change. The lightning strikes of the events of the story strike her feelings, and sadness invades her innocent face. At one point in time, tears almost fall from her hazel eyes.

The eyeliner was about to dissolve into the tears, drawing her feelings with its black lines running on her rosy cheeks, but she was definitely holding on and gripping her emotions flowing like a waterfall with an iron fist.

It seems that the suffering that the young man went through in his successive circumstances before finding himself on a path that satisfies him was really harsh and terrible.

But what she heard pushed her to follow her feelings, and finally she would find someone who would reciprocate her true feelings, which were expressed by (Azzam's) looks full of longing and admiration since the first meeting.

Rather, (Ibtisam) did not return to the bank as agreed with Mrs. (Salma). Rather, she called her and asked for permission to go home for an important urgent matter.

On the way, the voice of (Hisham), as he recounted the stories he knew about the life of (Azzam), manifested as an echo that filled the valleys of her ears.

Ideas are reflected in her thoughts, and emotions build the foundations of love without pressure. Perhaps her entry into his life now has a great value, as fate brought them together through a fleeting, innocent look.

Evidence emerges; its features are evident in her heart; she believes that he is tired, burdened with worries, and he is sure that he really needs her; and from another angle, she needs him in order to transfer the coldness of her life to the missing warmth, which increased after the departure of her father.

Contributing to her poor psychological condition, her mother (Fatima) surrendered to living in an atmosphere of sadness without any attempt to get out of it by any means; even her smiles became lifeless.

She was driving her car with a sullen face, so she did not turn on the radio as usual. She preferred complete stillness to surround her, perhaps helping her focus on what she intended to do during the coming days.

It is a decision she made out of conviction, and she will not back down in its implementation. The red traffic light stopped her, so she stopped her thinking as she looked at two people walking directly in front of her, and laughter spread around them, speaking in a loud voice with confidence.

(Ibtisam) got lost for a moment, and the sounds of car horns woke her up from her dream, so she moved slowly to continue her way, and as soon as she reached the house, she called the young man (Azzam) and asked to see him with great urgency that almost reached the point of begging.

As for the great surprise, he, too, welcomed the idea without any hesitation. His voice seemed to be playing words with a beautiful melody.

She threw her exhausted body on the bed, the desire to sleep haunted her, so finally she could get rid of this brawler called sleep, or so she thought herself, but she continued with her thoughts converging until the morning came from the window of her room.

She bets on his reaction to her request to see him and imagines how he will receive her sincere desire to be a part of his life.

She woke up immediately, and as a test called him, it seemed as if he was holding his phone and did not leave him to answer immediately. His voice carried a longing that could be felt, but the length of the conversation and the kind of flowery greetings remained steady and did not want to rush.

How amazed she was that at the end of the call, he completely got rid of any evidence of his longing and joy at being talked to him, and this feeling had a great impact that made her insist on overcoming all her shyness as a girl.

She ran out of the house, driving her car. The singer's voice added to the atmosphere, the required romance. Every moment that passed, she looked in the mirror and smiled.

She turns her hair right and left, then puts it back completely, takes off her glasses, and puts them on with movements that have already become funny to her. Even she became jealous of her teenage self.

She wanted to meet him in a restaurant on the outskirts of the city. It is the apprehension that a friend will see them. Perhaps this fear has gripped her since the moment the decision was made.

He was waiting for her at the entrance to the restaurant. She saw him smiling and walked over to him. He welcomed her. She extended her hand and greeted him, then they entered together, walking with the grace of butterflies.

In this restaurant, there was a large garden attached to it. They sat for a while around a table, the breeze caressing their bodies and hitting her face.

The locks of her hair move and fly, forming a magical sight that takes away his gaze.

Then they got up to walk together, carrying the steps of joy, and in the middle of the road, he finally impersonated the audacity, placing his palm in hers, and she seemed resigned, although she did not utter any word that gives him confidence that he is on the right path toward her heart that longs for him.

(Azzam) preferred to resort to silence as an attempt to encourage her, and the signs turned into light talk and laughter, followed by smiles that filled the place.

This revealed the soul of a person who is good at extracting happiness and who can make the road stones laugh if he wants.

He asked her if she wanted to leave, but she did not care and did not make him feel that her presence with him was a sign of something negative. She usually does not care and enjoys freedom that may sometimes lack discipline.

In the meantime, he used to argue that he was afraid of her, even from his own shadow. His tone was the sincerity, all gathered in an envelope written on it (I love you, Ibtisam).

How happy she was for this sublime human sense of feeling.

His beautiful behavior attracted her as well, which encouraged him to buy time and tell her frankly that he loves her since he laid eyes on her.

(Ibtisam) was listening silently, wandering in her imagination, when she felt a coldness in her body, and unfortunately, she bit her tongue.

Soon, she was getting closer to him, clinging to him as if she were a piece of his body.

His breath, full of heat emanating from the volcano of his chest, caressed her, and it was a wild desire that he wanted to kiss her when they entered the narrow corridor, and she felt it all.

The weather and the surrounding atmosphere colluded with the young man (Azzam), but he was afraid of losing her forever.

Or to show her the personality of a young, playful teenager who cannot control his overwhelming feelings.

And he falls harshly in a test of patience and honesty. He wanted her to enter his life, not out of the consolation that was achieved after what she heard, but rather out of a certain faith in the real feelings she carried for him with all the standards of love.

Before she left him and left, she asked him to share dinner with her at a new place downtown on the weekend, and (Azzam) agreed immediately.

But until that date, Ibtisam does not know how the days have passed. And why are her feelings arrogant in her unjust obstinacy?

She loves him, but she is afraid of a mysterious matter that may disturb this innocent relationship.

She preceded him to the specified place according to the previous agreed date, and his spectrum seemed to her from afar; he was elegant to an impressive degree, and the magic of love in his eyes.

She immediately asked him about the name of this fragrance coming from him with a force that steals her speech, and he replied with a brief answer that seemed sufficient to evaporate everything from hope or desire, so he said:

- It is the perfume that lady used to love.
- Who was with me all the time.
- She is the one who made me afraid to give you hope because I feel you.

She wandered away with the answer, and the features of her face changed suddenly, as she felt something that might tempt her to struggle in order to win Azzam and keep him, whatever details in his past might prevent her from loving him.

However, she was prepared to speak about herself for the first time without apprehension and without fear that would hinder the fulfilment of her beautiful dream.

It is clear that he did not need her to speak as much as he needed her to give him hope, which is difficult to obtain, and he looked at her carefully, scrutinizing the details of her delicate face, but despite that, she was apprehensive about his silence, which caused her calmness to be lost.

She wonders why he does not talk about his pain, which is forming in his eyes, as if he were a defeated and broken man. What prevents him and blocks the way of frankness?

Perhaps he has a different story for all that (Hisham) presented to her in terms of the details of his tragedy and the life of his misery, while calm seemed to him as he ate happily, that only (God) knows about.

It may seem that those moments of happiness disappear and radiate at times, and silence prevails in their conversations, which definitely contributed to the occurrence of apprehension and its return again, striking and shaking her calmness.

Here they are together having dinner by candles and the music is quiet.

She realized how human he was, although he did not make great strides in his education, but he was educated, and this did not require conclusive evidence to prove her assumptions.

But she took pity on him because he was in this way of pain and stillness sweeping his heart, and that renunciation comes out of him like a ray of dawn from all his stillness, movements, and looks.

Despite his feigned smiles, he tries to suppress the pain inside him, and it appears otherwise. This moment has no place for sadness, and he must give (Ibtisam) the happiness that he lost, and she has no fault in that.

Time moves on the rails of passion, and on board the two orphaned lovers sit, embezzling from time for hours that satiate their longing to say everything at once.

He was reluctant at first to seem like an anxious child with a girl of such beauty, innocence and tenderness.

For him, he was afraid to look like a reckless teenager rushing about, but with one look, he surrendered to his soul, and then he began to speak with the fluency of a poet.

And she remained happy next to him and sat in his heart, and with every turn, (Ibtisam) voluntarily gave him the opportunity to embrace her, even if this was just a fleeting dream in the events of the hour.

And you don't know why she needed it from him?

She realized, in a moment of wandering, how memories are formed that contain within them these delightful details.

She retracts her fear of the story and leaves herself to the man, whom she thought was a gift from the beautiful unseen to her, assuring that if he was absent, she would miss these touches.

The course of things is proceeding slowly, and between the clock hands aspirations live, for the young woman (Ibtisam), and if she surrenders to the rules of the present reality in which she lives with her being enjoying the pulses of her loving heart, she will not escape comparisons between his touches and the touches of others.

The imprint of his personality, if compared to those who will storm the coming days of Ibtisam, will drop them all from her accounts.

There is no real, fair comparison between him and them, as he really possesses her senses without a competitor.

Before he got out of her car, he told her that there was nothing stopping him from loving her, but that he might need to start a love story with her that the books would remember.

His faith drives him to her, that she is different from the rest of those he has lived with, but he certainly does not live in the world alone.

It is not the power that gives him the ability to impose his conditions on a reality of which he is a part.

Indeed, over time, reality will say its word that it is for him far beyond the stars of the sky, and Azzam in Ibtisam's life is just a very small part that cannot be seen with the naked eye.

At that time, she did not want to comment, as his fearful speech would change with a word from her, as she was the one who used to choose and defend her choices vigorously.

The space of freedom given to (Ibtisam) was greater than her mother's desire, so her mother asked her to explain to her the reason for being late this evening for this hour.

She is not used to being late before, as her daughter loves her, and this is the truth in the dress of detachment, and she has no alternative but to obey.

She loves that young man who suddenly appeared as an inevitable fate in a distinguished drama in the flower shop, with his strange and wondrous events.

And he is not (Hisham), who did not have the power for a moment to rob her daughter of her autism on the night of his mother's (Salma) birthday.

Rather, to increase clarity, her friend, with all her characteristics and her exposure to those who know her, is not the alternative model for her daughter.

She will not convince the young man or his mother, especially after it has become known to everyone that she has left the branch in which she works to work in another branch.

Perhaps his mother, Salma, meant by that decision to avoid (Ibtisam) the game of existential struggle and self-affirmation that those like her friend (Aisha) are keen on.

Or perhaps Mrs. (Salma) announced her decision to convey her personal opinion about her, as the young woman (Ibtisam) herself did not let time pass without thinking about her next step.

She knew her friend's intention and knew closely what she plans to do if she continues to work with her in the same branch. This situation will contribute to increasing the fires of jealousy, which will devour them all.

The young woman (Ibtisam) loves (Azzam), and the amount of sincerity flowing from his speech and his looks caught her attention, and perhaps he forgot his old sadness for her sake and he pretended to smile so as not to harm her, and in fact, he is the one who has the decision to choose.

Her sister (Ahlam) left with her husband, and she left her in the most difficult times, and compared to her, she may be more realistic than her.

Ibtisam wanted to send her a message via e-mail, asking for her opinion on the story; for sure, she would not care about her sister's opinion if it turned out to be the opposite of what she wished for.

However, she wants to see those who are realistic and free from the classical views that are concerned with social differences and are keen on the stability of social concepts.

It was very surprising that (Ahlam) did not stay long in her response. She knew how much her sister feels toward this young man who suddenly stormed the castle of her heart.

As soon as she received it, she rushed to send her opinion on the whole matter. She indicated, in a brief message, that (Ibtisam) is free to direct the feelings of her heart to whoever she wants and desires.

Therefore, the current and somewhat confusing circumstance requires her to choose as usual. But after saturating the matter with thinking and turning things around slowly.

Speed in this fateful field does not benefit at all, as much as it is beneficial to wait in digesting events with piercing eyes that have no feelings, because it is simply the first and the last that will alone pay the price of its choice.

However, something unfortunate happened, and against her will, it leaked to the social circle closest to (Ibtisam) that something had happened between her and the strange young man (Azzam).

The hints of Mrs. (Salma) during the bank's working hours exceeded the meaning of advice, reaching admonition from its widest gates. It is wise for her to separate her apologetic desires following what happened the day she entered the shop to buy flowers.

And she repeatedly advised her not to mix emotion with the course of events and their consequences, and the outcome of the events that developed to accuse (Azzam) of theft.

And the emergence of a relationship in the midst of these tangled circumstances may lead to the occurrence of an emotional tendency that may mean that there is a relationship about to begin.

Ibtisam's humanity moves her toward reactions that are not always appropriate, according to the opinion of others around her, and here lies her personal problem with them always. Despite the passage of time during which she remained a loyal friend to (Aisha), she never tried for a moment to confront her with her shortcomings, and she gained pity from her throughout her tenure. Despite the problems that afflict her, which stem from Aisha's jealousy of her.

However, (Ibtisam) believes that her friend (Aisha) would never have mercy on her for any mistake she made in a moment of human weakness, whether with good or bad intentions, and she will not overcome it.

As it happened on Christmas Eve, where her wish was to win (Hisham) on her own, believing that he will like her and prefer her over (Ibtisam), who is always silent.

The official (Salma's) talk about (Azzam) was not just a point of view regarding the information she received about a relationship that is about to start, but she, just like her son (Hisham), has a lot of information that pertains to this mysterious young man's thoughts.

But what everyone missed is that the story has crossed the anxiety of the beginnings for a long distance, and it has become as if he was waiting for the moment of decisiveness and the official announcement. Every morning, (Ibtisam) receives flowers from (Azzam) in her office.

As if by his actions, he is forcing her memory to not forget him, especially after his mother (Salma) dealt with (Ibtisam) by making her preoccupied to the point of drowning in work.

This arbitrary matter resulted in making her relationship with (Azzam) mere long conversations or short sentences over the phone, with him continuing to send a morning bouquet of lotus flowers, wishing her a beautiful day, so that she could meet him soon.

Most of the conversations during the hours of rest revolved around the person who surrendered to what happened to him in the past and how he received, given his young age, the meaning of others sympathizing with his suffering.

These details create split souls who have a clear-cut enmity with the world, which seems to their imagination to be unjust and does not deserve the suffering of engaging with it in order to defeat it.

Azzam is a complex case of people, and he is now observing the situation in one way or another. He works hard even outside the flower shop and through a small factory that produces many beautiful and expensive accessories.

But in reality, he did not get married and did not try, but when he spoke to (Ibtisam) the last time they had dinner, perhaps he referred to a story that happened in the past, and perhaps it left a shattering effect on his soul or deepened in him the legacy of old, often traumatic experiences.

It seems that (Ibtisam) at that time has surpassed these ideas, as she is the girl of this moment, he is sincere in his inclinations and his scandalous looks, and his personality does not seem like someone who messes with her or seeks to kill his emotional emptiness, and she, in turn, is not a frivolous or naive girl who is not good at understanding such a desire, so why does the past rule and shape our vision as we live now in all its details?

Concepts and meanings were changing in her psyche, between contentment with his feelings and her feelings, and between complete rejection of him and submission to what her social life dictates to her, as the situation is painful in all its stages.

(Ibtisam) has really become so tired of the lotus bouquets that she asks him to stop sending them, or, to be more precise, he gives her another chance to think if she decides to develop this relationship, and she is not fundamentally suspicious of her presence in his life or his presence in her world.

The only certainty in her realistic story is that he loves her and was not ashamed of declaring his love, despite his uncertainty of her feelings toward him, and this is a sign that she found in him a large area of sincerity for her presence next to him; in order for her to face the difficult and changeable world together, for him he sees that the challenge represented in the life of (Ibtisam) is the day she faces her world that she loves him.

She came to apologize with Hisham, but who is Hisham in his life? Hisham is the only person in this city who knows him well.

And if she asked him for advice, he would tell her honestly about the nature of the tragedy that he experienced with its real events, whether he was a distant orphan, and what happened to his half-uncles after the death of his father.

The stark social contrast will surround (Ibtisam) and put her choices in a harsh and difficult situation.

On the other hand, her mother, with the passage of time, used to think in the same way that Mrs. (Salma) thinks, as she is not really motivated about the social class to which the young man (Azzam) belongs.

Although most of his family is wealthy to some degree, they are not interested in him and his small family. Where is the secret in that? And why do they alienate him?

And he, in turn, may have some savings that may help him appear in her daughter's life as an ideal husband that she is proud of in front of everyone.

Rather, it is more honest that the reality now recognizes that the disparity in academic degrees is no longer a matter that preoccupies the thinking of families of this era who secretly pray for the marriage of their daughters; money may be the tyrant leader in most directions.

The logic in the new love story was the one who drew its picture in front of the eyes of those around them. The relationship between (Ibtisam) and (Azzam) has moved forward, in which feelings are growing.

And the focus of their thinking became a lack of interest in the opinions of those who see the impossibility of things developing between them or interpreting them in an interpretation that does not belong to anything other than pity for him and human communication that is free from any other purpose, in which there is little foothold for love.

All those close to the new story were impatiently waiting for one of its parties to announce the final decisive moment, the moment of enlightenment that they were talking about.

The relationship has reached the utmost maturity, or is barely reaching, as they cross huge waves that they have no precedent over, so can they cross them to reach the shores of total happiness with their meeting under one roof?

While it was clear to everyone who followed the events of the story that whoever knew (Ibtisam) closely knew that her life with the entry of (Azzam) had changed and changed significantly.

The area of her former silence has receded, and she seemed to come to life more, like a bird jumping on the branches of joy with joy, singing her dreams openly without fear or apprehension in the morning.

Thus, the mills of conversations began to rotate among those close to her, and rumors arose that she had forgotten her grief, whether about the shocking death of her father, or what was reflected in turn on her mother (Fatima) from the repercussions of this death, or even that imposed absence that (Ahlam) cruelly implemented without a clear reason, with the certainty that her travel was to fulfill her scientific ambition.

As for what is going on in the mind of (Hisham), who lives with his mother, Mrs. (Salma), he was simply following the situation from another angle, as he was watching very carefully from afar the news of (Ibtisam), of course.

And what is certain is not like a potential lover, but he became her friend and closer to her brother, and she was, to be honest, seeing this meaning in him with remarkable clarity.

It is fair that (Ibtisam) admits at this time that her boss at work has not changed her manner with her, especially when she was certain that she had succumbed to her strong feelings and loved the person called (Azzam), despite all the apparent social obstacles that might prevent the love story from continuing. And reaching happy endings, as is the case in most of the romantic stories of lovers throughout the ages.

However, Mrs. (Salma) seemed to send to the gentle young woman (Ibtisam) all messages of reassurance that she is sure that she is on the right path with her love for that young man, because her normal instinct can understand the areas of good and evil, and that she and (Azzam) will inevitably achieve a good picture of a successful relationship.

Given the obvious optimism about (Ibtisam), Salma tried to invest in the parallel life she was running while also attracting her mother under the desire to get her out of her grief.

The life of Mrs. (Salma) away from her professional cadre was characterized by multifaceted gifts and forms in social life on both the personal and public levels.

This is what revealed to (Ibtisam) that her boss is fond of voluntary work and even appreciates charitable work greatly and gives it all her life's interests. It is also noticeable that the boss does not hesitate at all to follow the path of everything that is useful and good for the society in which she lives.

Although she belonged to a financially secure family, her large family was somewhat wealthy, so when she presented the idea to (Ibtisam), who in turn passed it on to her mother (Fatima), she found great encouragement.

To form together a humanitarian institution in charitable works whose goal is to provide assistance to those who need it within the limits of what they can achieve.

It is strange that this step had a great impact, which turned the life of the beautiful and kind girl into something like a complete preoccupation.

Which made (Azzam) feel from time to time that his beloved (Ibtisam) undoubtedly started the path of her new life without him having a place in it, and this was certainly not true but rather the opposite.

The gentle girl (Ibtisam) was honest with herself, and she did not go beyond what was destined for her, that the fates of those like her always surrender to their destinies and feel weak despite the hardness of their souls.

In order to get her share in life, she will not only need to watch in life, but it may also be necessary for her to engage with life in an open struggle, in which she sometimes uses all weapons to achieve aspirations.

And from this human logic comes the drama of changing events that breaks the boredom and monotony of the day in which people live.

The young woman must be patient for a long time and look a lot at her mother until she sees the impact of this qualitative shift in her daughter's life, which saved her from the clutches of grief that almost destroyed her at the time of her surrender.

Perhaps (Ibtisam) exaggerated her preoccupation with the details of her new life, which is ramifying and filling her emptiness. She was drinking the cup of loneliness in silence, while trying as much as she could to maintain her contact with (Azzam), the absent present.

But she was feeling happy, and she would not have intended to lose that happiness for any reason, so removing misery and sadness from the lives of others is a mighty work that deserves sacrifice, so how will her lover receive the events that occurred in the life of his beloved?

Those thoughts were successively fluctuating in her mind as she watched the situation closely.

Also projecting mistakes on others is (Azzam's) eternal ordeal. This characteristic has infiltrated his life since he was a child, and he is hanging the course of his life on the peg of the life of misery, his companion.

It is not easy for a young man in his circumstances to admit a mistake, as he sees that people are the ones who make mistakes and mismanage, even that small group that sometimes deliberately ignores him.

And it is just a feather with which whims play. Azzam's place is always in the human sentence is the object of a subject who is not good at planning the future.

Although (Ibtisam) had confided to him the secret of her absence and the regression of her appointments with him, he did not feel reassured, so he remained anxious and felt that her kindness did not want to announce the end that might hurt his heart and that hope would collapse and die under its rubble.

Here is the ambitious young man. Every night he used to sleep on a carpet stretched from the thorns of obsessions and suspicions, so the ceiling of his bedroom seemed to show strange scenes. He regretted himself and said: ("Why do I not forget my obsessions, so I leave them amid indifference?")

Then he returns voluntarily to the fact that Ibtisam is the love of his life, whose fortunes will not let him down to get her in the end, no matter how long or short it takes to achieve his hopes suspended between heaven and earth.

In a coincidence designed by fate, he meets his friend (Hisham) in one of the shopping centers. To be honest, he realizes the honesty of this man, so he directly raises his fear for (Ibtisam). That fear that may take the form of worrying about his relationship with her after Ibtisam was completely preoccupied with him, or his fear that life would consume her while she is a delicate girl who may not bear her hustle and cruelty.

In fact, (Azzam) kept leaking these meanings to his friend until he found the correct explanation for his fears, and in turn, (Hisham) called on him to continue his life normally, to get out of his isolation and change his lifestyle that led to the interruption of his communication with his old acquaintances.

Azzam no longer has the old passion to leave his private life, and if it is related to the young woman (Ibtisam), the only fact that does not accept any doubt is that she loves him in all circumstances, places, and times.

There is no benefit from loneliness, as it destroys hope and topples the bridges of aspirations, so (Hisham) notices that his friend has lost his old passion and hard work, and he no longer wants to leave his private life.

His friend Azzam has become more surrendered to him, outside the world of reality, as if he is searching for a lost wish that will not return, and if it is related to his beloved (Ibtisam), the only truth is that he loves her despite the alleged estrangement.

This phrase from the friend (Hisham) had a beautiful effect on his psyche. His facial features changed, and his usual smile appeared immediately. The words were like magic after they came out from Hisham's tongue. Azzam felt satisfied after he felt some doubt that Hisham was his rival, but Hisham is an honest person.

Over time, Mrs. Salma had the greatest impact on Ibtisam's life at this stage, especially when she began expanding her charitable volunteer work.

Soon, her reputation spread in the district, and the women of the neighborhood knew her as a good lady of the first class, and with her this kind, smiling girl who deals with her world with great tenderness, love, and great sympathy.

In this very complex world of people, people with weak souls may not be able to correctly explain the behavior of (Ibtisam) and her boss in life.

Difficulties pour in and problems multiply, carried by the folds of negative comments, as it helps to spread some sick, abnormal mouths.

It is the life that refutes events according to what he desires, not interested at all in kindness but rather considers it as a mere sympathy intended to obtain reputation with a few dirhams.

Perhaps the presence of the name of the rich (Ibtisam) in the context of this noble humanitarian goal did not pass peacefully to many of her relatives.

Her participation in charitable work with Mrs. (Salma) to achieve the humanitarian goals of the needy, oppressed, and miserable of life was nothing but a losing card for her.

What will she do with the ever-fluctuating social conditions? How will she deal with ideas that do not believe in change?

What is remarkable is that all the people surrounding her with decisive certainty know her family and the exceptional standard of living that she has reached.

Likewise, they never lose sight of the history of her father, the shrewd merchant, and they also knew who this problematic girl was, whose name and biography people were repeating with the passage of time, as she does not lose sight of their thoughts almost throughout the day.

Those intruding people on her and her family did not know the secret of the muffled apprehension that tends toward her and her movement affected by it, as she is just a good girl who only wants to provide the required help and assistance to those who really need it from among the people who live in the shadow of life and its fierce cruelty.

Indeed, (Ibtisam) was sensing these successive concerns that were trying to extinguish the light of her life, so she rushed to throw them in the way of Mrs. (Salma) as if she was begging for help.

Who knows, perhaps she will find something to remove this hostile feeling from some famous businessmen in the city regarding the services they provide that need their moral support before the material one.

There weren't many blank spaces in the context of the information originally in Mrs. (Salma's) mind since she began her charitable activity with the help of (Ibtisam), so she would not care what was said at all.

Everyone, since she entered the bank as an ordinary employee, has been dealing with her with admiration mixed with fear, as she is an exceptional woman who sets the high-end, arrogant model for the ladies of the city, and her success may arouse the wrath of the senior employees of her competitors.

However, she did not care much about what people say with their tongues when they collide with models that they sometimes call them with epithets that may seem positive, and they say: ("extreme idealism"), and many times they accuse people of foolishness because of their different, reactionary ideas.

Since she was advanced in age, she began to take this charitable activity for the sake of people. They used to say that she lives outside of time, and she does not know anything about her world except what she is living today.

It is the conflict of materialism that is hateful to some and beloved to others, and it is the frantic strife to accumulate wealth in its four seasons, so that two women like (Ibtisam) and Mrs. (Salma) become an actual exception.

They seem to have descended from outer space through a cosmic time portal, or perhaps by means of a flying saucer, crashing into our home planet.

(Ibtisam) was sighing in a moment of contemplation in the presence of the present fighters in the battle of life, so she smiled at them and said to herself, whispering to her thoughts: *(Unfortunately, we no longer see the rich looking diligently for the poor in order to offer him a hand of help and assistance).*

So where did doing good go? And where does the feeling of sympathy for the poor hide in the minds of the wealthy?

As usual, she began to think of giving as a talent that most likely needs perseverance and practice and not as a point of view that pushes a person to be generous at certain times only.

Rather, he must always be generous and not be moved by satanic tendencies, and he exercises his positive moral feeling on those who really need help and no one else.

So this young woman started practicing her life with the ideas she believed in. She went out and entered the house, saluting her mother (Fatima), who did not leave watching television, which became a close friend of her thought.

However, the strange thing is that this mother does not express any comment when she learns of some of the inconveniences that her daughter is exposed to while practicing the new, unique work.

Yes, he is unique and new to her wealthy family. Who believes that earning life does not come by relying on the donations of others and nothing but other work, but she is sure that her daughter loves this volunteer and humanitarian work, which in turn is consistent with her dreams in childhood.

Those dreams that she adopted in order to support the poor and teach them what benefits them do not want a financial return or an emotional return as much as everyone appreciates her sacrifices for the happiness of the needy.

She also realizes that her daughter (Ibtisam) is a loyal girl to what she learned and heard from her father. Her father was never late when he heard that someone needed help.

And often he was victorious for the dignity of the needy, and even often he communicated with him at night without waiting for him, a victory for personal pride that might be affected by the giving of generous people and their bestowing favors on them.

Her father often held collective breakfast parties during the days of Ramadan for workers coming from other cities, and this was always his practice, so he was overjoyed when he broke his fast with them.

He shares their meals with them, as there is no boss or subordinate in those spiritual meetings.

And he used to say to her always: ("All I want from them is their good prayers that there is no veil between them and (God), and this is how blessing descends on us, because they are the secret of the success of my business.")

Her good-natured father believed that these people were nothing but victims of the difficult circumstances of life, so it was enough for them to feel the growing oppression in their hearts because of their lack of family in such a month.

Therefore, it is necessary for us to gather everyone at one table, as this would soften this feeling of loss, especially during the days and nights of Ramadan.

The giving characteristic of (Ibtisam) has always moved with the mere knowledge that there is a person who needs a helping hand in order to pull him out of drowning in the bottoms of the garbage, so that strange tendency among some members of rich families follows a very special point of view, but rather they believe in it with the utmost faith.

She believed that money is a temporary thing in people's lives and that it is just that the mind of the rich should focus on this human meaning, so when (God) increased them abundantly in wealth, he wanted to test them before he wanted to increase their livelihood.

Only people in this universe follow the reasons that may lead them to obtain sustenance, but even this sustenance itself, no one can obtain it without God's help, and no creature ever controls it.

And she began to remember a wealthy man in her father's time who used to sit with people and say sarcastic words such as: ("If poverty were a jet plane, he would never realize it.")

He was seduced by his growing wealth and that he was the one who collected it with his own hands and shaped it without the help of anyone, and he did not praise (God) for the blessings that God bestowed upon him.

Rather, it was arrogant that he did not hesitate to slap the poor if they extended their hands to ask for help; rather, he used to call them thieves of the rich's sustenance!

And she remembers that she was with her father one day, and he entered with her at the house of a man whose features were the basis for the misery accumulated on his face, and his appearance was disgusting.

People have turned away from him, and he is sitting alone, sharing his worries, motionless, in deadly calm. He was waiting for the flood of generous people who belonged to the old days, and her father was one of them.

Her father used to break into the man's misery and secretly give him an envelope of money to meet his needs, in addition to some necessary medicines that he needed to maintain his life and, with them, help his exhausted body to fight diseases.

And when they left him, she knew that he was the man who was mocking poverty and saying that he would never realize it with his jet plane! So did he achieve his goal?

Tyranny of money on people is an ordeal that people cannot bear the consequences of, so whoever grants wealth, no matter how great it is of diamonds, gold, and silver, can easily take it away in a blink of an eye.

Indeed, (God) is the Lord of causes, possessing the absolute power to grant or deny, and her paternal grandmother, who resembles her (Ibtisam), believed that envy was a form of disbelief in the greatness of the Creator.

And her mother (Fatima) objected to the harshness of the analogy, so she justifies the Grandmother and says that her description is that the envious person does not believe that there is justice that runs the world, so why do people envy each other?

And there is a compelling force that practices giving without any injustice to anyone and according to the great wisdom possessed by (God), the just Creator of the universe.

People, according to her opinion, are mere mediators and nothing more. Perhaps they do not own anything. They are only entrusted with this money, and perhaps what destroyed the world and put it in that unfortunate position is that some of the rich believe that there is no moral or human obligation that determines the form of the bilateral relationship between the rich and the poor. As they are two sides of the same coin is human.

And who knows, perhaps these meanings of moral values are what prompted the young woman (Ibtisam) to establish the form of her relationship with money in this manner of thinking.

She certainly has nothing; she only guards the money in anticipation of those who need it, to extend a helping hand to him as much as she can, but she will not be able to continue giving if the needy person does not practice a job that provides him with a living before anything else.

It has also become certain that (Ibtisam) suffers from embarrassment that strikes her at the core of her heart when she meets others, because the model she adopts is not easy for people to accept, or perhaps those around her in the rich society.

Between declared accusations of misbehavior and others implicitly accusing her of folly and extreme extravagance, she is not more merciful than God, who created the poor, as those discouraged and mercenaries in human moral values say.

Some of them may even accuse her of fighting destinies as Dankishot fights windmills, so if (God) wanted, he would have made everyone rich without exception, but she never stopped at these false and unfair accusations that come to her directly or come to her as a hint from those who do not want to hurt her because of their excessive love for her.

Everyone agrees that this young woman will sooner or later not be able to realistically meet the needs of the needy and distressed, as with the passage of time the money will run out and the wealth will disappear little by little.

And she will be in need of asking for help and assistance from others, so has she really forgotten this realistic perception? Or is she just arrogant?

Regarding Azzam's life, he was unable, due to his excessive time constraints and the distribution of his activities, to express encouragement to her in these circumstances.

For example, to offer some help may mean, at worst, a moral gain in her heart.

He only loves her and sincerely wants her to love him too, but unfortunately he did not explain her preoccupation other than that it was a temporary truce in order to make a decision about his presence in her life.

But this meaning continued to hurt him throughout the period of waiting in groaning silence. He himself had fallen into the trap of interpreting the wrong things that were against his beloved, sometimes unfair.

A girl in her circumstances, why is she rushing after money? Perhaps in the coming days she will not need it, or perhaps luck betrayed him on the day they met in one of the places.

The conversation, which seemed warm and gentle at first, arrived; to take the form of a trial for her life since she began her new charitable activity.

His justifications were harsh for her life for the sake of others, so his thoughts overthrew every hope she had in her mind toward him.

And the matter became even more difficult when he publicly accused her of suffering from emptiness! And his presence in her life, from his point of view, was enough for her to not live that feeling of emptiness and to deprive him of his rights as a lover while she was running after Mrs. (Salma).

How realistic the meanings and allusions seemed to her, for she did not think that these thoughts, even in a disturbing dream, would be material for discussion with the man whom she loves with all her being.

Especially since she is a girl with a distinguished education, she carries in her inner certainty what indicates the meaning of the sublime human message in all its details and believes in it, and she will never give up performing her humanitarian message.

I have read about the life of (Tolstoy), the great Russian writer. I learned that the man owned farms of thousands of hectares, which he distributed to the poor peasants.

Even before the Bolshevik revolution succeeds and establishes the socialism of society as a whole, human conscience often precedes theories, those written on a group of papers with ink that fades if a drop of the sweat of the toilers falls on it.

And when she finished talking to him, she caught a glimpse of a smile that she had not previously seen on (Azzam's) face.

A smile from which Ibtisam was pained crushed her thought and distorted his beautiful image, but she immediately pulled herself together, got up jumping off the chair, put on her glasses, and her smile seemed to hide hurt feelings behind it.

So she said goodbye to him, following his concerns through his conversation with (Hisham) when he told him that he believed that he might be the only person in her life.

Perhaps fates lead my feet to her. My night has become an orphan. Looking for her spectrum while I walk between my paths alone…

The Night

On her way home, suspicions started collapsing in an unimaginable way; it was tearing her soul, and she was wiping away every moment of love she spent with her lover. She did not expect that smile full of mockery of her personal ideas,

He thus allows himself to be the sole controller of it with absolute power and refuses to have an inviolable independence.

When (Ibtisam) entered the house, she showed signs of dissatisfaction. Her mother read those expressions of total dissatisfaction by giving a quick greeting and directly going up to her room, racing against time.

Her mother did not want to interfere and follow her to her room to clarify the reasons for those broken looks filled with drops of tears that refuse to fall and for those deep emotions emanating from her grim face.

That night was one of the most difficult nights. Ibtisam tried hard to sleep, but she was unable to do so on the first try.

She was as if delirious from a fever that had swept her. She was pulling the cart of questions, wondering why those people believed that she was fighting fates.

And she only believes in something that exceeds her individual sense of the taste of grace, as human and moral responsibility will not enable her to enjoy money.

She realizes with certainty that there is a group of people who cannot sleep because they are suffering from hunger. And they do not find anyone who brings them treatment to fight diseases.

Rather, it is certain for her that there are also those who do not find anything to eat except through garbage bins in this modern city, which is full of names of people who are on the front pages of wealth undisputedly. Their pictures adorn articles with bodily poses that reveal unwavering self-confidence.

She also knows that there are houses that imprison between their walls huge sorrows that are closed to their owners now, and these people hardly sleep from the tingling of hunger that kills their stomachs filled with fresh air only.

Or there is a child who no longer goes to school because his father did not bring him a pen or notebook to write his wasted wishes on.

The picture is much more difficult than those rich people who are wrapped in their solitude in remote, luxurious dwellings think, so that these provocative and painful scenes do not harm them.

Then how could the love of her heart (Azzam), with a story of bitter struggle, deny her sense of sympathy toward others? Wasn't he also at some point in dire need of that sympathy and human compassion at a time apart from his miserable life?

Or has he deliberately forgotten those circumstances in order to be arrogant over them by force?

Days passed and the last meeting of the two lovers was thrown into a sea of oblivion, and (Ibtisam's) smile became just a dream lost by (Azzam), drowning in remorse between the anvil of self-reproach and the hammer of fear of facing the truth.

The lover realized too late how harsh he had been with his beloved. With all his spontaneous tyranny, he did not pay any attention to her thoughts, even if it was just a courtesy that counts as a kind of required emotional hypocrisy.

He is usually not arrogant, even in the narrowest circumstances when he has proofs, and voluntarily admits his mistakes when his angry soul calms down.

But he will remain a mere human in the end, unable to control the totality of his feelings, and what will he bet on if he abandons his fear of her thoughts and presents himself as a lover who is infatuated with his love and nothing more than that.

He began to wonder, as the distress tightened on his nerves, suffocating him: ("What will I say to those who follow my life despite their scarcity? If I let her suffer from a vacuum that I formed with my behavior.")

Then he thinks what the fault of this tender girl is in falling into the abyss of choice; for her, Azzam was the most difficult choice she encountered.

How can she relate her life to a man as soon as he puts forward a different point of view about what his beloved is doing and finds that her features have changed, as if he is seeing her for the first time?

While on the other side of the river of lovers, (Ibtisam) still lives in confusion, gnawing at her thoughts.

Since she entered her room after that vague conversation with her lover and in the first meeting with the mirror, she was shocked by the shape of her features, which did not express her happiness about this, the development of her relationship with the man.

The man with whom she was keen to talk for as long as possible, and who will be the trustee of her treasures of secrets, protecting them from the hands of dream thieves.

How exhausting the night devil is for her to think again, repeating the conversations of the last meeting without getting bored, so she tries to resist him by all means, but all of them fail, so how can she manage her affairs?

And what would the intruders say if they realized she was occupied with a man who was so paranoid about what she was doing, and she thought he'd be proud of it.

Thus, throughout the coming days, she began to wish herself that he would present his apology on a platter accompanied by a bouquet of roses and then begin to clarify his ambiguous position toward her thoughts.

She wished that his affectionate voice would come to her to sing to her the courtship poems with his usual tenderness. Those nightly obsessions were robbing her of her sleep, and the night was accompanying Ibtisam with his shadows, tracing the light of the lit candles to extinguish them.

Darkness prevails throughout her room, and she drowns in fear of the unknown and moves on in the hazy circumstances.

In the eyes of the two lovers, love is not a state of weakness, but rather an implicit waiver of one thing or a great meaning to another that is equivalent to feelings, that whoever we want deserves it voluntarily.

And as long as fear has been demolished and the convoys of passion chants are marching to play the heartbeat, there is nothing less than that her lover exchanges his feelings for what is greater, but on the condition that he understands them clearly.

But thinking of a turn like this is an unforgivable betrayal for her in the shadows of these volatile events, then why doesn't she directly admit that she loves him so much? Also, since when does she give weight to the opinions of others?

They interfere with advice or comment on a matter of her private personal life, and their opinion is nothing more than an air bubble, and she will never accept their intervention, even if (Azzam) the love of her life is the perpetrator?

It seems that (Ibtisam) has returned to the same difficult calculations that prompted her to evaluate who seeks to propose to her according to what nature has bestowed upon her from the elements of a beautiful girl, who must link her fate to a man who definitely deserves to enter his bosom to sleep quietly and fall into a deep slumber with the melodies of his heart.

She does not look like someone who condescended until he embraced her with that warm embrace, because at that time he would be more human than her and her burning feelings.

Suspicions are not lost; as usual, they come and go like the movement of the ebb and flow when the waves of the sea hit the shores of thinking. She smiles at times from her childish actions, and at other times she collects the remnants of longing so that dreams do not leave her.

The beautiful thing is that the child (Ibtisam) did not accuse (Azzam) of a lack of understanding and cruelty. Through her constant preoccupation with him, she made this.

She pushed him to be impartial with her to the maximum extent and kill happiness. He was waiting for a word from her that would give him the security he needed throughout the days of her absence, but she did not and will not, so why is she looking for him now? Did she believe in the strength of her love and desire for his presence in order to start another new life with him?

(Azzam) does not know how these days passed, rushing in a hurry to implement their worldly affairs, but this emotional emptiness shackles his soul.

And the repetition of defeats kept crowding his thinking, so he was consumed by cups of bitter coffee without reaching a decisive decision.

She was able to easily control the moment with its details. She did not give him the impression that she had rejected his ideas. She seemed expert and successful in containing him and gave him hope with a confidence that made him ashamed.

He often never betrayed those who trusted him, nor did he carry within himself the aspirations of a young man who seeks to kill time with denial. It is not easy to search for justifications to explain his sincere feelings toward her.

He was frozen, paralyzed, and his heart was in a far corner, with no place for him in the game of days he lived in the midst of the jungle of worries, but Ibtisam arrived and persuaded him to change immediately.

So why does he swim with her inclination toward him against earthly gravity, for reality will not have mercy on him while he is manifesting to amazed looks that follow their lives together, and they know the clear chemistry of the difference between them.

His fear of being associated with a beautiful, tender girl appears at a dead time, and feelings trapped between the walls of the past, which will abort this hope tainted with tension and confusion hanging over him.

If his nature was to escape to the amusements of life, he would have said the facts and did not hesitate to narrate them, or is there something else in the matter that he could not disclose in front of her for fear of the consequences of her feelings being destroyed.

With this act, he wants with conviction to remove suffering from her at any cost, so it is enough for him to drink from the painful and hard-to-forget setbacks of life.

The reality of the difference between them does not need compelling evidence. She lives in an environment where dreams are realistic, and he lives in an environment that lacks dreams. This is the secret of his fear of being associated with a girl of childish beauty, and tenderness.

She entered his gloomy lair at a time when there is no life, like a barren desert, which will certainly contribute to the miscarriage of their dreams.

Why does (Azzam) tend to enter publicly into a battlefield of conflict with fates? But with this provocative behavior, he contradicts himself, because love at that time, as he sees it, is not linked to the categories of luck, sharing, and destiny only.

Thus, he announced what he felt through emotional expressions and began to tell those close to him, as if accusing her of being unfair to him. Love is a free decision that will not be subject to the scepter of the heart as much as it involves complex calculations.

Some thoughts visited him in the evening, before going to sleep, and settled on the deceit of the lonely deserter.

To draw with these ideas clearly the shape of the conclusions and endings for him and her in a relationship based on the logic of the need for a young man and a girl who have the luxury of choice and desperately resist the monsters of reality and the predators of traditions.

He admits in his silence while looking at the ceiling of his room the pain of thinking in this way, asking the surrounding darkness: *("Where is love?")*

He turns with his tired body to the east, looking through the open window in the distant sky, and there is a star that twinkles, and he smiles reluctantly. Then he talks to her, calling her; perhaps she will send him solutions because he is the one who lived on the flood of his feelings.

How does life turn into a static, cold drawing made by a feather made of stone so that it does not give intimate moments their burning meaning, and love resists asceticism in pleasure and gives life it's crazy and beautiful perceptions.

But that young woman was trying hard to tear down the walls of stagnation and the frost that has come to surround their relationship, and she admits that they feel the amount of pain from this deadly distance of feelings.

So she resorts to her thought, imploring him to play his role with ease, not being disturbed by anyone, fearing that he will be defeated, so thoughts visit her in parts of the night, but she hastens to grab a writing feather to write her thoughts in her pink notebook, then in stillness she surrenders and soars with dreams.

She used to sleep and wake up to his memory as if he were her inevitable shadow, so how is the way to forget him when he was the one who stirred her emotions with his charming looks and charming smiles, attacking her mind and robbing her mind without asking permission.

These meanings have contributed to her quest to return to him, despite her fear of his thoughts. May he surround her with his love so that she can return to his heart.

On the other hand, where events in the bank proceed in a monotonous manner, each employee performs his work according to the directives, and the new circumstances did not change what Mrs. (Salma) believed in.

She does not resist the idea that (Ibtisam's) condition does not bode well at the present time, as everyone who watches her knows how depressed and sad she is when she smiles at them.

What really makes the situation more difficult is that some of those who work with her began to claim that she impersonates this state of misery of her own free will. They also admit that there is a story and there are heroes to it, and there are circumstances that animate the play of love.

But who are the main characters in each scene, who turns the situation around and messes with the pictures and changes their colors?

However, Mrs. Salma seemed a bit confused. She did not think that this kind and affectionate girl, who is moved by the reality of every moment, is evidence of her being strong. So it falls like a feather, carried by gossip, or like a weak doll that is thrown over a cliff from which it is difficult to escape.

Or is there some hope that conditions will change due to an actor who appears suddenly to change the course of things, so who could be this person who will save her?

It is inconceivable that this cheerful, intelligent young woman does not know, until this moment, and with the certainty of the motive, that she is unable to move away from the ghost of (Azzam); his shadow haunts her while awake and asleep. It is love in its purely human meaning.

Or does Mrs. (Salma) agree wholeheartedly with the ideas of her son (Hashem) that she is still lost among the mirages of suspicions, running after them, and finds nothing but loss and that she wants things that are difficult to define.

She is always busy establishing dreams that may be bigger than her; she sails with her in a sea known as the abundance of storms; she leads her life skillfully with the testimony of everyone; even those who hate her ideas trust her abilities.

However, her relationship with (Azzam) may have been affected in light of the developments in her private life and her complete consumption of her time in running to fulfill her wishes.

When she sits with herself, she feels that (Azzam's) decision to stay away from her carries a veiled insult toward her, and it was clearly too realistic to go beyond reasonable limits, and she is a beautiful girl who has a broader view of the future.

So what prompts her to boldly build her life and begin with it with a young man who may realize that the feelings of an orphaned man at that time may, in fact, seem strange to him?

Love has become a commodity whose stocks are driven by the laws of supply and demand. Even the ideas themselves have become a commodity that is bought and sold. The values that he had been talking about throughout his life as universal principles became suicides before his eyes and united with being a point of view.

What drives him to exhaust himself in order to adapt to her world or to her perceptions that she is trying to project onto reality, including his own humanity?

It is certain that (Azzam) has realized her extreme idealism, and even if he went with determination to weave a relationship with her with silk threads, transcending the problems of his life, what are his motives, especially in this difficult time with all its details and suffering full of pessimism, and will (Ibtisam) really appreciate his sacrifices without knowing the reasons ?

As for the difficulty in implementing her dreams, it lies in the fact that she is the type of girl who likes to show feelings in an overwhelming flow that does not stop flowing in the groove of love.

The most difficult thing is to keep their relationship behind the barrier of traditions while they are trying to fight it by rejecting it. Can they succeed in deciphering the dilemma that everyone who tried it lost despite its human legitimacy?

From time to time, Mrs. Salma used to talk to her son about Ibtisam's crisis and its developments, while he listened to his mother's explanation and did not stop thinking about her condition.

He often urged her to be patient in her flowing thoughts if she was anxious and afraid for her life.

Whatever he does to support his mother's perceptions, (Ibtisam) is not in this ideal human sense that lies at the bottom of extremism.

Perhaps she is haunted by the confusion of the connection between the father who has suddenly disappeared, and that beloved, whose greatest desire is to sleep in his lap with peace of mind after a long torment.

There is no crisis, in its explicit sense, experienced by this ambitious young woman greater than the logical reconciliation between these contradictory and painful ideas from her point of view.

He realized during his conversations with her that she knows with certainty that in this life it is difficult for a person to defeat his enemies with just a single decision that he makes without reviewing his detailed results, which may be harsh on him as much as it is harsh on the suffering of his enemies.

She, too, told him, in a moment of serenity, that love might be able to eliminate some of the prohibitions on the road, especially if it was kindled in the hearts of lovers, igniting the fuse of enthusiasm and the powder of giving, and its only weapon would remain mutual respect between lovers.

But she was sighing silently as she told him, with groans flowing from her throat, that it seemed to her that it was her bad luck that she had met (Azzam) and that she felt sorry about that!

If she thinks about her as much as one gram, then he also thinks about his affairs to the point of committing suicide! He will not bear the looks of people who may accuse him of robbing the girl of her dreams and kidnapping her.

Nor do they accuse Azzam of taking advantage of her need for the love and strength of a father who was forbidden by fate to be near her, and he will never have patience with those who think that he only trapped her in his love.

It is not easy to bet that there are those who see love and have removed all human differences and barriers, and even bless them for this beautiful and impossible human connection from his point of view, at least in such intertwined circumstances.

Whether it was on her part or he was the one who fabricated it, which formed their contradictory social world before they met together on the shores of life.

Here are the fates finally, which enable (Hisham) to meet Azzam at the entrance to the flower shop, so he seemed to him tired and had many signs of fatigue shown by the dark circles surrounding his eyes.

Azzam wanted to escape from his gaze and hide among the bouquets of roses, to disappear like a small lily that has no power.

In fact, (Azzam) was not happy when he saw (Hisham) coming toward him, so he welcomed him and then entered his office with him, and immediately, without introductions, he started talking about (Ibtisam), and how she was in his abhorrent absence.

He did not need to tell him how much she loved him, but he appeared with a face that he had never been keen to show, with sad features and apprehension covering his face, to reflect a state of great, unique love and greater fear.

Suddenly (Hisham) got up to embrace him and said, in a tone that was closer to pleading than begging: ("Give your beloved (Ibtisam) the opportunity to be in your life regardless of any expected breakage between you.")

Believe me with certainty, there is nothing to lose, neither you nor she, but suddenly he was hurt by this hilarious proposal, and he started saying that he is not one of those young men who kill time with free feelings, so either he loves her or she is out of his life forever.

(Azzam) opened his heart to let out the pain of his love and admitted that the memories of his old failure hinder this loving connection to himself.

One needs a girl with a degree of innocent childhood feelings, whose tenderness pulls him with the threads of memories to bring him back to his previous worlds, those illusions that removed from his life the meanings of love.

The power of ambition in Ibtisam's eyes is greater than his ambition in this world, which has become a great rivalry with everything he desires from it.

Since his father died and the hardships of life embraced him, until she gave him her miserable sympathy on a plate studded with the lost, she used to water him every evening and morning, feeling the bitterness of the struggle for someone who did not deserve.

She also impersonates boldness and will not bear the attacks of fierce questions, as she is certainly looking for the authority of a father who was suddenly absent from her life by death, or for that bosom filled with narcissistic feelings, to contain her for eternity.

Or perhaps it will not coincide with his tendencies rejecting that world, and his personal tendency to seek to be in a cocoon of his own, and not be a mirror image of others.

The incident may have been a mere coincidence, as one morning (Ibtisam) was passing by the flower shop, her heartbeat was getting louder, almost out of her chest. She was walking at the pace of her shyness, and she was resisting the feelings coming from the longing that carried her legs to enter the shop.

And in her cheeks a redness formed, which was exposed by the rays of the sun falling on her in their golden color, while (Azzam) was standing behind the glass in a manner approaching a wandering into the world of oblivion.

Despite all the longing she had to see him, even if it was a fleeting glance to extinguish the flames of longing, she remained arrogant, and the strange thing is that she does not know the reason, because she is fond of his ambiguity that hurts her feelings or his provocative personality.

She lost the answers, and she is searching again for his lost tenderness. He has possessed the keys to the heart, and the fear is that the keys to her happiness will be lost from their hands at a moment that people consider a game of interests.

She does not deny that in the last conversation that brought them together, she was terrified of the loss of aspirations. The reason may be the lack of logic in her actions. Either he believes in them or he has reservations, and he must be frank with them.

And before leaving the place completely and moving, she called him and kept watching from afar, so she saw him taking his phone out of his pocket, but he stopped in front of the screen and did not answer.

There, perhaps, she decided to withdraw temporarily so that she would be the first to take the initiative in the imposed boycott of the love story, whose papers are hidden in the chest drawers.

But she went back to asking, from the reality of her obsessions: *("Why the estrangement as long as she loves him? And this is an inevitable fact.")*

The young woman (Ibtisam) was burdened with many worries throughout the days of the week, and these concerns did not leave her mind; she no longer tolerated conversations and preferred solitude; even the music became lonely for her; nothing in the universe was beautiful in her eyes.

These defeated feelings, in turn, were reflected in her features as she provoked Mrs. (Salma) to ask her boldly about the developments in her relationship with (Azzam).

She did not know with all realism and competence what to answer her, so she seemed to confess in an empty room to someone who could not be identified; she was afraid to open the issue with her mother, and she would certainly tell her an opinion that inevitably called her to end the dilemma.

From what I have heard from her mother about Azzam's suffering from psychological compounds from an old tragedy that a young man lived through, but it is reasonable that Mrs. (Salma) would dare to tell her logical and correct opinion, as she is very aware of her experiences in life.

The description of the desperate look of need that she found clearly in his eyes is conclusive evidence of his extreme admiration for her beautiful presence.

However, in the light of the last meeting, she wanted to remove the claws of his crisis, as it became clear from his words the meaning of defeat from the world, a defeat that makes him shaken and dressed in black.

And she wanted to urge him not to forcefully ignore her personal thoughts without thinking with certainty, and that he should support her with his heart, mind, and human being before others play these heroic roles.

While he is standing watching outside the game, why does he disappoint her with his actions and never tries to go with her in achieving their dreams?

The strange thing is that everyone who knew her story with him sincerely advised her to give herself a warrior's truce and withdraw temporarily from his life quietly and without painful fuss.

But despite her conviction of what is said about the momentary controversy, she soon returns to her first feelings that gave her confidence that he will accept all her rituals without reservations and regain his confidence with a little patience.

And in light of the current circumstances in this time of moods, where the hypothesis of the ideal personality disappears, it is not easy at all to meet a man who convinces you effortlessly that he is different from others with that simplicity of expression.

At a time when society celebrates shocking and boring stereotypes, we are forced to live with them in their human qualities by coercion and share life with them.

Since her heart chose him among the men around her, she was clearly aware that he lived alone. He lives in his shell so that he rarely goes to his family's house, and for her, this matter may be conclusive evidence that he wants to get close to her.

But, unfortunately, even this did not happen. It was enough that longing would push him to accomplish the desire to get closer, and why would he be late while she was sitting on the fire like a princess burning from the flames of raging love.

(Ibtisam) used to admit before the court of conscience that he did not properly receive the developments of her ideas and the radical changes in her life, but despite all the sharp collisions with his views, she continued to respect him and appreciate his innate favor because he did not lie.

Ibtisam was clear with him from the first moment, and she confirms that his social life and family circumstances prevented the completion of this step at the present time.

She repeatedly tried to give him the ideal solution to get out of the scourge of the psychological pressures he was facing. It became wise for them to change the pattern of the current relationship, but he did indeed seem committed to a certain moral commitment toward his family in need of him, especially when he recounted experiences that seemed difficult to her, and in some of their events may be beyond imagination.

Her crisis with this model of men was that there was no room for doubt, so he always forced her to believe him, whether by speaking or by looking. Experience taught her to look into the eyes in order to investigate the truth from lies without exaggeration in emotions.

The truth is that (Azzam) was never lying; even when she offered him love, she did not choose the right word.

She began to remember the situation in its details and live with its groans, but for a moment she stopped thinking and realized that she had said to him: ("I love you, and I want you in my life.")

The harshness of the blatant expression of sympathy became evident only when she saw his face, which had completely changed its color.

Immediately, the looks of admiration also disappeared, and the warmth vanished, and in its place resentment and disgust appeared, and he hastened to immediately stop the outpouring of grief.

And at that crucial moment of their love life, she felt as if he wanted to scream out of the intensity of anger that suddenly overtook his feelings, and it was clear from his facial expressions as if he wanted to say to her: ("Leave out of here.")

But he kept clenching his nerves tightly, almost tore them to pieces, and became disciplined until he looked at his watch in disturbing silence, then quickly stood upright, asked permission to leave, and uttered a few words in his mouth that did not exceed good-bye.

And before he disappeared, she would reluctantly adopt a childish reaction formula in which passion intensified despite her desperate attempts to deny this fondness, wanting to test the extent to which she had offended him.

When it seemed as if he was going to disappear among the human crowd, he suddenly stood up and turned his face toward her, looking at her and speaking to her. Immediately, she took out a handkerchief and placed it over her eyes, as if to dry her tears.

Until this moment in the life of waiting, she does not know what the fates hide for her and how he boldly crossed these meters and came to sit attached to her body like a shadow of his anxious longing, not interested in his act and his daring with all the looks that surrounded them.

He puts his arm on her shoulder and his face, as if he was about to kiss her, and began to regret. Is he simply apologizing? Or is it just a reaction that circumstances ably brought about?

It seems as if he was affected by her crying with a strange sincerity that she did not expect, and the young woman (Ibtisam) inside her feels an overwhelming happiness that she had never felt before.

He called on her to pray (to God) on this night. In order to remove everything that hinders their desire to be together and their wishes come true.

And here she is now drinking the cups of confusion alone, the circumstances have become greater than her ability to bear, she wants with conviction to continue, but it is the fear of curbing her enthusiasm and controlling her emotions.

She sighed deeply and silenced her conversations successively, while Mrs. Salma remained perched on her seat in astonishment that hindered her tongue and thought, as if she could not find anything to say.

On a summer night, the longest boredom in his new life, Azzam's sleep was interrupted by a transient nightmare filled with terror, so he felt when he got up in a panic that he was breathing through the eye of a needle.

He was run over by a huge bus that shattered his body, although he was running from it trying to avoid it while it was madly trying to seek his certain death.

When he went back to sleep after reciting some Quranic verses to help him, he felt some relief in his body, but he did not sleep and began tossing and turning like a wounded bird falling into the sea.

It seemed to him that the ceiling of the room presents strange scenes, through which he follows the events of his life in its final circumstances, and in each scene the spectrum of Ibtisam appears, and he extends his hands to caress her.

Perhaps it is the reality, but he comes to his senses and says: *("Why don't I forget what I lost and surrender voluntarily to her love.")*

The days and the details they carried between the folds of their events did not foreshadow the truce between them. Which some advised Ibtisam to live with, with what appears to be a collision between two trains running at a crazy speed over one line and directly toward each other.

This is the actual explanation of the state of her thoughts on the one hand, and the opposite of his thoughts opposing them.

But what really hurts her heart is that he lost a passion the follow her news; perhaps he thinks that she is really living in a state of truce that may precede her final and fateful decision for both of them.

Either she will continue to love him or she will disappear without leaving behind anything that causes grief for her loss.

This is, of course, impossible to happen. Where (Azzam) will not be arrogant, and he will confess with obedience that her departure from his life is a tragedy that his soul will not dream of. He really loved her, and he hopes that his life will end with her.

In this escalating time of events, where hearts fluctuate between acceptance and complete rejection of the entire facts.

What (Azzam) did not realize is that the drama of life that he knows has reached the point of merging into it as soul and body.

He gasps behind obsessions and looks at things with a hazy eye, despite his experience in life. His thoughts betrayed him in ways that could not be counted, so he fell out of the dictionary of assumptions that the same coin has two sides.

In the upcoming events of his life, he is destined to pay the price dearly, especially when he comes to his knowledge by chance in the coming days that his tender sweetheart (Ibtisam) has been struggling with many strange ideas about her velvety society and social status, and the repercussions that rain calamities.

In addition to other things that are absent, and he will greatly and bitterly regret that he took the flimsy assumptions of him through a false choice.

The Test

In a strange surprise that only exists in movies, her sister (Ahlam) arrived with her husband and their son. She did not stay at the father's house, but she preferred to stay with her husband's family (Sultan).

This behavior affected Ibtisam's psyche, and she was not happy with this visit, especially when she learned that it was short, not exceeding a few days.

And the conversations started that she only wanted the Grandmother to see her grandson and then go on a new journey.

But it seems that (Ahlam) felt that her sister (Ibtisam) was not well as the signs of change in her life and her nature became clear to her.

She was like a butterfly living in the fields of her dreams and persevering to fulfill her wishes calmly and deliberately, and now she is very busy running behind a mirage that represents her expected love story, and she is interested in trivial things, which in the past she did not pay any attention to.

It was an exceptional moment from which the sun of facts does not miss, and it must be taken advantage of at any cost, so it was necessary to ask her about the latest developments in her relationship with (Azzam).

Ibtisam spoke about him in a long letter that she had previously sent to her sister, Ahlam, in order to obtain a decisive opinion from her and help her with solutions to her story, which is intertwined with threads of events.

As for the strangest and shocking thing at the same time, when I told her that the story had stopped her scenes for reasons that did not include the disappearance of the feelings that she was and still carries for him.

But he shocked her when he heard her new ideas; since she entered and participated in the work team of Mrs. Salma, her boss in the bank, especially those related to charitable and voluntary activities.

Ibtisam gave her a brief, semi-detailed summary of the story of Azzam's life, which is full of turns of misery and deprivation. That story she heard from

(Hisham), the son of her manager (Salma), and he himself confirmed its events when there were many interviews between them.

She spoke with a burning in her heart, as if she was asking for relief from her sister (Ahlam), as a last attempt to help her search for definitive solutions.

Her sister has always been a good advisor and showered her with useful suggestions, being more inclined toward actual reality than her, far from her rosy aspirations and dreams.

(Ibtisam) was resolutely denying that the one she loved had been exposed to disgraceful childhood details that might have affected him.

Or those details left in him what indicates the meaning of the complex psychological complex, but he seems to her very surrendered to what he believes and does not accept the opinions of others.

She was moving imperceptibly, roaming around her room, stopping at the window, looking at the street as if she was waiting for an obvious event, then continuing her speech in a voice of pain, saying to her: (He is indifferent to my personal inclinations, and he compulsively imposes immediate submission to his demands if I love him, without giving me the right to choose, so I fell as an easy prey. between his thoughts and my dreams).

The situation was not easy for her and her sister, who knew in advance that she would suffer severe suffering, to reach the height of patience to implicitly reveal to her that life had brought her with (Azzam) to a crossroads.

And the delinquency of this dangerous and fatal turn is whether or not it is a legal sentence that I memorized by heart, written by (Shakespeare) and pronounced by (Hamlet).

But the most difficult thing in the whole story remains that her lover (Azzam) began to retreat on his own and no longer sent the lotus bouquets that he used to send, as if he wanted to possess her feelings.

The time it was sent gradually decreased, from day after day to a bouquet every week to almost no flowers.

After she finished her speech, she asked her permission to leave immediately. It may be that the events imprisoned (Ibtisam) in an ivory tower, from which there is no way to get down except through a resounding fall from the highest point.

Ibtisam settled on the ground, a lifeless body, that famous scene in the stories of the two lovers. When the heroine decides to end the chapters of her love, her hope at that moment is to wait for her hero to come to save her from bad fortune and harsh circumstances.

However, it seems that she retracted her decision to leave after repeated urging from her sister (Ahlam). She sat down, sighing, and then continued the rest of her extensive speech.

She told her that her contacts from him had become few, and she feared that his passion might have also declined, believing that she was preparing for a decision regarding her life with him or her life without him.

However, the movement of destinies that formed after that gave the story twists that most pessimists would bet on happening.

(Ibtisam) hurried to sit near her sister and immediately began to open the tablet computer. Then she became very enthusiastic about flipping through the pages, folding them in her hand.

Her intention is to give her an opportunity to view the Facebook account of her lover (Azzam), and her ultimate moral goal is just so that she can look at him to make sure of her matrix proofs.

Ahlam, who was searching for a specific meaning in this fleeting visit, was not preoccupied with reading the thoughts of her sister's lover or discovering a surprise that was not taken into account by his interventions.

But what caught her attention was that he was last seen months ago.

What is also shocking to her is that many of those who know him publish what indicates their concern about his continuous absence, and this meaning was really confusing.

This is a moment of waiting and anticipation that engulfed Ibtisam's mind, as her sister did not say a word.

Her thoughts invaded her calmness, so she surrendered to those thoughts, so she was struck with confusion, which got out of her control like a child, and she started running to search for conclusive evidence that would erase all this pessimism painted on her forehead, which clouded her entire features.

A surprise of a heavy caliber turned that calm upside down when their mother (Fatima) entered. With this entry, the cord of their conversations was severed, and the flow of their thoughts was interrupted with it.

They looked at her with some discomfort, which was evident on their faces, but they could not tell her anything legal to prove that she entered at an inappropriate time.

Her words hurried to tell them that dinner was ready, and they accepted the reality and got up together, walking behind her, and the looks did not leave the immobility.

At the dinner table in the family home, her sister (Ahlam) eagerly asked her about the developments in her new life in charitable work and what she heard of the active activities she was participating in with Mrs. (Salma).

It seems that (Ibtisam's) immersion in her emotional crisis made it as if the sister had thrown a jug of ice water on her head, which froze her senses.

It seemed as if there was some strangeness in her mind about accepting her. Neither the manner of the question nor the appearance that her sister (Ahlam) impersonated was comfortable. Rather, it seemed as if she was one of her sworn opponents.

The people who do not hesitate at all to attack her, to finally accept reality and surrender to their opinions, is the feeling that overwhelms her with apprehension, forcing her to resort to silence in order to pick a shocking answer for everyone that refutes the ideas of those who besiege her in her personal life.

(Ibtisam) was suffering from those who berated her biography with their stinging tongues, spouting mockery through her yellow smiles almost throughout the day.

She did not know the secret of the hidden hatred in their chests, which turned toward her alone, and followed her movements in the context of her being a girl who wanted to make something for her own world.

and as an interjection sentence that overturned the balance of logic, (Ibtisam) announced to her sister that she would not stop, or at least she would adjust the form of her relationship with the issue of spending on many humanitarian cases that she adopted with Mrs. (Salma).

Not for fear of losing wealth, but she has returned to her childhood time through this work, and her spirit when she does so is characterized by lightness and a love of altruism.

From the first moment, she was shocked by her amazing speech, sentences, and the vocabulary proved the sincerity of her feelings. The life of (Ibtisam) for (Ahlam) was provocative to anyone who noticed the form of her relentless movement in life.

Talking about this matter has become unbearable, especially for the camp of the rich, and the truth is that the intelligence with which it dealt with these circumstances deserves praise.

It was not hidden from all the people who knew about her sister (Ibtisam), who was immersed in the depths of suspicion despite the clear love in her eyes, and that she had transcended the idea of giving in its traditional form and was now in the process of institutional work to fully integrate into the entity of institutional work in her spirit, as she goes as a visitor in the cover of the night; to give anyone she knows needs money to help them cope with a difficult life.

Just as she was certain that she had traveled with her thinking mind beyond financial giving, she realized and believed in her father that money alone will not help the poor to overcome his crises, no matter how much cash assistance is.

Money for a poor person may represent a palliative pill that crosses him from accidental pain, but it will not give him full health later.

She believed that she should look into the capabilities and talents of the poor in the region, for surely there is no person without ability and talent.

It is better for her to help him to earn his own living as much as possible, with a firm certainty in his mind that does not rust with time, until he ends his pain and realizes his ambition that brings livelihood.

Since that moment, Ibtisam has transformed itself into a limited economic institution that is not concerned with helping the poor only, as much as it is keen to make them move from the ranks of the destitute to the rank of active producers in their society and not really differing from the rest of the members of society in all aspects of life.

It is that growing feeling in souls who believe in their abilities and that they have the skill to attract money, no matter how difficult their circumstances are and how miserable they are.

The voids were multiplying with surprising steadiness in the context of the information that certainly existed in Ahlam's mind. Her thinking did not stop as an attempt to decipher the mysteries of her innocent and kind sister. With her adventurous spirit, she refused to be referred to as the usual model for girls of that era.

However, despite her falling in the destined love, she failed in converting him to a new life, and she enjoys his help.

For the first time, Ibtisam seems drawn to something fateful with such bias.

For her part, the sister tries by all means to inquire about the whole matter and its details from her mother (Fatima).

Unfortunately, she did not find an answer as much as she found the same reservations that she raised about Azzam's complex human past and psychological structures with authoritarian reactionary ideas.

It seems that this mother refuses to talk about him, as if she is convinced that he is the wrong person who entered the life of her kind and gentle daughter to tamper with her fate.

On the other hand, her sister, Ibtisam, cannot misinterpret her feelings with such bad judgments.

Perhaps she wants, through distance, to test the loyalty of the one she loves, with the availability of reasons that may prevent the continuation, even from (Azzam's) point of view, at least.

In his isolation and unjustified distance, he may see things from the same eyes as his sister (Ahlam) or her mother.

Will this volatile young man accept the imposed estrangement as if it were part of the nature of things?

Or will the voice of his heart triumph over the cacophony of his heart and try to change for her sake?

But until now he did not think about it as (Ibtisam) wished, and the evidence for that is the incident that shook her sister's feelings and plunged her into the bottom of the well of delirium from the severity of the shock.

Ibtisam mentioned to her how his shocking reaction to reality was when he saw their name on his phone screen and never responded, as if he was announcing from his position that the ball is now in her sister's court.

And from afar, he takes the approach of someone who waits to see, analyze, and judge together, so he decides together. His decision may be sudden, and she will not bear its consequences, and as a result of her delicacy, she may suffer a major setback.

In fact, the gentle (Ibtisam) was not harmed by these gratuitous conflicts that occurred on the sidelines of her love for (Azzam).

She stands for her humanity above all else and also stands for the meanings of true giving that she adopted throughout her life.

Therefore, she will not be satisfied with raising the flag of surrender easily for the sake of the love that entered her life at a moment that was one of the happiest moments that passed through her loving heart.

It is clear to sister (Ahlam) that her sister reprimands him as a matter of reproaching lovers only. It was necessary for (Azzam) to understand as long as he loves her that she is only his.

And the world around her is just a field of social activity that gives meaning to life without causing him disturbance or loss, as obsessions establish a pressure of suspicion that has no place.

There are many women like Ibtisam. Lying does not agree with their sincerity, but they feel the way, and they want a model that can crystallize their aspirations to work and mix with society in an effective, positive, and fruitful manner.

Perhaps this meaning (Azzam) was not aware of in order to answer the question that he did not need an answer from, so why is he surprised by what (Ibtisam) does, especially since her personal freedom never harms him.

The time of conversations between the two twin sisters extended against their will, and the days passed when the hours diverged and the hands of the clock converged.

And one day (Ahlam) reminded her of the publishing house that she had hoped to establish after her graduation, and she was afraid of confronting her late father with this idea due to the excessive distance between that activity and his commercial activities.

Perhaps (Ibtisam) remembered this distant desire coming from the depths of the years and those days of memories of the private exemplary school that the family would undertake to establish after the death of their father, and the idea was thrown into the trash awaiting its fate.

The train of enthusiasm has passed, so she will work hard again in order to achieve it on the ground and at least fulfill her father's dream and restore his consideration with an ideal that has no impurities.

Her sister also told her that the matter only requires her to take all the audacity of a tyrant to achieve it, and then she was silent, waiting for her sister's calm reaction at this moment.

It seems to her that she has strayed while she was with this idea that (Ahlam) brought to life in her speech now.

And she only expressed her satisfaction with a sentence: ("We may implement it after presenting the idea to Mrs. (Salma). As for me, she has a great deal of good behavior, has her experiences, and will not be stingy in helping us.")

She closed her eyes to that brief intervention, and her sister watched her behavior, a bit surprised, so their conversation suddenly ended as it had begun, and (Ibtisam) fell into a comprehensive state of fatigue and sweating.

She wanted to get up, but she could not, at first she explained that she was tired and with some painkillers or surrendering to sleep, she would rest when the morning of a new day would come.

At this hour, (Ibtisam) forgot that her sister is a doctor, and she certainly would not believe what her sister had told her of only passing fatigue. She kept watching her with suspicious apprehension as thoughts turned in her mind like pages.

She is looking for a satisfactory answer to what happened to her sister suddenly and forced her into absolute silence, so she tried to make her sister comfortable, and after an hour, the attempt did not work.

Fatigue and exhaustion clearly appeared on her yellowed face, and there, (Ahlam) realized that her sister was more than just a state of stress, especially since (Ibtisam), according to what she heard from her mother, did not know rest in these old days.

Rather, it was running in all directions, striving hard for the needy in their area, and this may lead to physical consequences that do not have unfortunate consequences over time.

Ibtisam's fatigue was like a state where she was about to fall from a fast-running horse. She was never able to get up except with the help of (Ahlam), who was surprised by this matter that befell her sister.

She suddenly appeared so weak that she could hardly walk straight, and excruciating pain prevented her, for her legs could not bear her.

Her powers betrayed her at this moment when she desperately needed them to complete the difficult task.

She hurried to extend a helping hand to her sister, so she accompanied her to her room on the upper floor. Fortunately, there was an elevator in the house, which their father had ordered to install three months before his death.

When she entered, she lay on the bed, her limbs cold, her eyes yellow, her face pale, and her voice resonating between her teeth, hidden behind her completely closed lips.

The night passed, and anxiety spread its concerns in the big house, and scenes of apprehension spread throughout its vast rooms.

Everyone is awake and sleep is looming, but sleep refuses to give them inattention to keep their eyes open.

Even (Ahlam) was turning over the embers of suspicion, trying to sleep next to her husband and her young child, who were sleeping peacefully.

And when the morning came and the sun's rays filled the big house, no symptoms of relief appeared on Ibtisam's face.

Even her body seems to have refused to obey and get up. Here (Ahlam) hastened to call Mrs. (Salma) telling her immediately what happened to her sister.

This lady was the closest to her, and she would certainly not hesitate to provide the required assistance in such humanitarian circumstances.

Indeed, within an hour, Mrs. (Salma) did not come alone but came with (Hisham), her son, and panic was evident on her face, and sweat was pouring from her face.

(Ibtisam) tried to control her fatigue so as not to worry them about her current health conditions, but the signs of extreme fatigue were greater than her failed attempts to manage.

Rather, it caused all of them at that time a confusing shock that they never expected to happen. It paralyzed their thinking and let down their fear for her when she asked them directly about the news, conditions, and location of (Azzam), and she forgot most of her fatigue.

She indicated that the story between them had stopped temporarily and that they had agreed to find a space of time that would allow them to make the right and frank decision without hurting the other with the subsequent consequences of their lives.

On the banks of ideas, (Ahlam) was sitting, waiting with extreme caution, hoping to believe that it was really a matter of fatigue or accidental fatigue and nothing else.

And that the main reason is the exaggerated effort made by her sister for a while, forgetting to take care of her health and her skinny body, despite the presence of many concerns warning that the matter may be greater than this after the color of (Ibtisam's) eyes changed and became completely yellow.

Her concern stems from the fact that the occurrence of intermittent bouts of coma may mean that the story may have definitely started from the liver, especially since liver problems take a genetic turn in this family, according to medical studies.

In order to refute these doubts, medical analyzes must be conducted as soon as possible, for fear that things will escalate, God forbid.

**I hope that my wish will grow in the deserted lands of my beloved.
I am not afraid of the distance for sure, but I will water it from the beating of my tender heart so that it grows...**

Disease Ghosts

When fate surprises you with its details, you often realize how great the calamity is, and the test this time is greater than what (Ibtisam) or all those close to her expect.

In a symptom that started as a simple pain that represents nothing but tiredness and exhaustion, to many tests that showed serious fatigue, at that time (Ibtisam) learned that she was suffering from a disease in the liver as the disease came and did not want to leave her exhausted body.

The condition, it seems, from the initial examinations, may seem serious, and it is better for her at the present time to seek treatment abroad immediately without delay, which would deteriorate her health condition for the worse.

There is therapeutic medicine that has made great strides in the field of treating liver diseases and its cultivation, if necessary, through surgical intervention.

The experience of (Ibtisam's) illness was a significant difference that exceeded all perceptions, whose colors were imprinted on the morals of those who dealt with it.

Everyone who knew about her illness was immediately affected and expressed concern and annoyance that exceeded her anxiety about what she heard from the doctors who dealt with her sudden illness.

But with the heart of a believing girl who is submissive to the will of her Lord, she received the developments of her illness with a calmness that was witnessed by Mrs. (Salma), who was in her worst psychological condition when she knew the condition of the sick, tired young woman.

She really felt her suffering and felt her delicate feelings, and in a moment of despair, she almost cried in front of her, but she behaved well when she asked her permission to leave to cry alone in the elevator without supervision.

Rather, she tried, during the past periods, to finish everything she dreamed of quickly, with the help of every tangible and unparalleled effort, and also in one go, before her health condition worsened.

Unfortunate things happen that impede her well-known efforts to continue, and this matter negatively affects her world.

Obsessions emanating from her anxiety, which she took for herself as a battleground that breaks out between the mind and the heart, between abandonment and closeness to a lover who finds it difficult for her to decipher his confusing love poems, and between her ideas that she believed in despite the successive difficulties.

So why does it seem as if she will surely die when she is nothing but a sick girl who needs to prepare to travel to receive treatment and not prepare to leave life.

Ibtisam dealt with the matter of her going abroad to receive that crucial treatment for her pain with racism and strange anger at the beginning.

As this raises a great controversy among the people close to and surrounding it, some of whom are in favor of the idea and some of them are opposed to it, medicine in her country is not so bad and ugly.

Perhaps she was convinced after deep thinking that contributed to confirming it and giving her the ability to clearly understand things.

Her sister, Dr. Ahlam, has supported her opinion of respecting the competence of doctors in her country and their role in providing the required effective treatment.

But with regard to her current medical condition, it is better for her to leave quickly to seek the help of doctors abroad due to the development of treatment for similar pathological conditions.

The specter of Ibtisam leaving her mother was really killing her and adding fuel to the fire of separation. It seems clear and without a confusing doubt that her sister will soon return with her husband due to the lack of her vacation time with him.

And this matter is the highlight of implementation, as she walks with him wherever his travels land, and she is unable to argue with him according to the data of the current family events, despite his prior knowledge that her sister (Ibtisam) will leave and their mother will remain suffering from bitter loneliness due to her absence.

The usual questions were constantly hitting her mind with huge waves of suspicion. Who will manage the life of their mother (Fatima), who has only left a few months from the prison of her old crises?

Indeed, getting used to life next to Mrs. (Salma) and her noble dreams has reached an insurmountable amount, but her health this time is the thing that changed the way of playing and the movement of chess pieces by force without the existence of the ideal, alternative, convincing choices.

Everyone around her knows that she will soon leave her family, not for tourism or for a leisure vacation to wash away the pain of her successive troubles, but it is the disease that seems dangerous despite the insistence of those around her.

They say to her, repeating in their good hearts, that it is a simple disease and that the world has finally found the final cure for those who suffer from it.

Mrs. Salma was entrusted with Ibtisam's secrets, and she did not tell anyone from the close circle about the truth about her illness.

With her usual experience, she used to deal with the phenomenon of her absence from work and from the management of the charitable association throughout that difficult and critical period, and she closed the issue of her absence as soon as it began by publicly forgetting about it.

She also began to talk about other topics by entering the corridors of other topics, the intention being to distract people as much as possible.

Thus, she moves away, and in her feelings, rains of sadness fall behind the walls of her broken heart, so that her son (Hisham), in turn, did not and will not convey the developments of her health condition to his friend (Azzam) as well.

As for the son, he sees with certainty that the one who was absent surrendered to his ideas, in which there is nothing true in them. It is not wise for him to return now to any of the meanings of compassion.

Perhaps Azzam believes that the absence of his beloved (Ibtisam) was due to Ibtisam abandoning him, but she is now suffering from an incurable disease that may affect her, so what is the point of revealing her illness to him?

The feeling of sadness was heavy and increasing in the hearts of everyone who loved the gentle (Ibtisam), including her mother and sister as well. These are feelings whose basis is humanity at the peak of her actual giving.

However, the movement of fates when designing a drama does not care much about calculations. Mrs. (Salma) was betting on this white rose through her belief in the next hope, as she bet that she would triumph for herself from any possible blackness that wanders in her life and their lives alike.

Basically, (Ibtisam) was suffering from a lack of friendships, and her continuation in helping Mrs. (Salma) was nothing but an expression of this meaning, a feeling that dominates her thoughts.

This lady was thinking about the situation of this tender young girl and finding many of her dignified and noble attitudes, and she judged them by the logic of her experience in life and her coexistence with people of different social levels with different ideas and the multiplicity of opinions.

So when she thought of announcing the secret, she was thinking out loud with (Hisham), her son, to dare and tell her close friend (Aisha), who, as soon as she moved to another branch of the bank in which she works and was sure that (Hisham) would not marry her, she completely turned away from Follow Ibtisam news.

Rather, Aisha also did not communicate with the official (Salma), who had the greatest impact on her career in the coming days.

The resounding surprise was shocking to the entity of the friend (Aisha), when Mrs. (Salma) called her, not only did she want to have intimate contact with her but also told her that (Ibtisam) was not feeling well.

(Aisha) did not understand at first what was meant by this brief phrase with great meanings, but she soon moved directly to her friend's house while she was driving her car quickly.

This call disturbed her and created an unbearable void in her soul that only reassurance will fill.

As soon as she arrived and went up to her owner's room, she did not control her emotions at all. It is a complete breakdown, overflowing with tears.

The picture was terrifying to the point of terror for the eyes of the girl, who would not have thought, even in a disturbing nightmare, to see (Ibtisam), the beautiful, radiant with such fatigue, who referred her old friend to a mere specter of a ghost that almost resembled her.

Perhaps (Aisha) was crying for the first time without her known discipline, which made everyone who followed the scene ask her to stop immediately.

Because that sad, revealing crying of feelings may break her friend and make her feel that the matter is very serious, and this is greater than what she thinks about her health condition.

For the friend (Ibtisam), she never imagined that the situation would be so serious, and what her friend is doing is only a hypothetical human expression created by her illness and supported by her strong feelings.

But Ibtisam did not hide her surprise about this strange and somewhat surprising visit to her, as her friend (Aisha) does not have those feelings that ordinary people practice.

It was only from her that she looked directly at Mrs. (Salma) in clear admonition.

But she soon returned cheerful to this visit, so she finally smiled reluctantly, struggling with her anger and calming the spread of her thoughts, as the situation does not allow that.

These behaviors did not indicate intentional anger. Thus, Mrs. Salma quickly realized what she meant from those quick looks sent from her eyes, accompanied by the volatility of her features. and support from her eyebrows.

They are messages that do not need further explanation for those who understand those like them.

Despite all the exhaustion and fatigue tinged with some pain, they sat talking for a long time about the reproaches of friends, talking about that stage in which there was no news of her.

And when they were alone together, she told her about that young man whom they accused on the day of Mrs. (Salma's) party of stealing her bag, and they brought him the police, who revealed his innocence of this act.

Immediately, (Aisha) remembered him and realized with the continuation of the conversation that between her friend (Ibtisam) and him there was a beautiful love story that was not devoid of suffering, and now she is suffering from an unjustified interruption.

But he is still in her heart, although it is possible that he has gone to believe that she has left him and gone on with her life paths, and lives without him.

The friend could not control her raging feelings, so she quickly offered her to intervene personally in the matter, but (Ibtisam) rejected the idea altogether, threw the proposal into oblivion, and asked her to wait until her health improved.

Then there are other things that could happen; this is so that the story continues sailing with its dreams or stops completely, swallowing the fate of the consequences of the abhorrent separation and the cemetery of the two lovers.

When (Aisha) went out to the hall, leaving behind (Ibtisam) in her bed, she was surprised to see (Hisham), who in turn was surprised by her presence in reality.

So, out of anger, he looked at his mother, considering that she had misbehaved because of her insistence on the arrival of (Aisha), especially after all that had happened from her in terms of estrangement.

She no longer asks about her or (Ibtisam), believing that they have agreed to get her out of the bank and out of their lives completely.

(Aisha) was able to intelligently read (Hisham's) looks correctly. She told him that when she moved away, she did not accuse anyone of having hindered her presence in the bank next to his mother.

She didn't go as far as to think that (Ibtisam) was in love with him. Since the incident of the flower shop, she has realized with a female instinct that that young man has controlled her friend, Ibtisam, through his feelings.

As for her, she was weak and resigned to her often suspicious way of thinking, and what prevented her from continuing her friendship with her was that she was weaker than facing her kind eyes, and she is in that way of envy because Ibtisam has a greater impact on her and is always able to be consistent with herself and others.

So, she did not think carefully when she learned that her good friend was not feeling well, so she immediately decided to take advantage of the opportunity that she had been waiting for a while to correct the course of her disgraceful actions and what she said that deserved punishment for it.

Then she wiped with her palm those fallen tears, drops on her cheeks, washing away her thoughts.

Her looks have tenderness, and her speech is full of tenderness. She decided to restore the rope of affection after it was severed by unjust concerns and to take advantage of this opportunity so that things return to the sincerity of feelings and not to illusions.

The time has come for her to open a new page with everyone and to give them pure love, which is equal to all that her friend (Ibtisam) gave in terms of giving and affection throughout her cohabitation with her.

Perhaps Mrs. (Salma) won her bet on the bright and radiant part of the beauty of the character (Aisha).

Here are her sincere feelings coming out successively after she was imprisoned in the prison of stagnation that she imposed on herself in order to live in it.

Her kindness was manifested in a way that she had not thought of since she first saw her at the bank; her voice was ruminating with sadness as she valiantly resisted her suffocating and painful expressions.

There is no greater and deeper sense of evidence than Ibtisam's mother embracing her for her kind and honorable presence at this critical and difficult time that her daughter is going through.

On the other hand, was the meaning of the tragedy created by her friend's illness the thing that rediscovered (Aisha) for herself? after she was absent in the journey of unjust suspicions.

And this meaning of feelings seems to have changed many things in the certainty of (Hisham), who believed everything that (Aisha) said from the words that clarified and manifested her condition with all boldness and did not stand in front of her words that she revealed in front of everyone,

With emotion, sadness appears, and transparently expressing her gratitude for the fates that made (Ibtisam) her only friend and revealed to her the truths hidden in the fog of ingratitude.

The moments were drowned in the turmoil of circumstances, and to avoid this sad surrounding weather embodied in the gloom prominent on everyone's faces, (Aisha) entered again where (Ibtisam) was lying, asking to follow up on Ibtisam's health condition and to obtain the results of the tests and x-rays that were conducted on her diseased liver.

At this stage, opinions are unanimous in these cases, and it is wise to hear the opinion of medicine or a point of view based on laboratory reports and analyses, and there are no exceptional alternative solutions.

No one stands in the way of the analysis and denies it, as it does not lie or hypocrite.

Despite the absurdity of this desire, after (Ibtisam) became sure of the truth about her serious illness, she decided to give her the opportunity to be an active person in her crisis, or, in other words, to give her the opportunity she wished to erase the traces of past mistakes.

Ibtisam did this so that Aisha could return again as a close and loyal friend whom she loved, without the social hypocrisy linked to the power of money before anything else, which tarnished the image of the beautiful friendship with the colors of flattery and false morals.

It was clear that the night did not end in peace, not for the heart of Mrs. (Salma), who may have rediscovered the metal of her friend (Aisha), which was hidden under the mud of the remnants of her confused psyche.

Nor from the mind and heart of (Hisham), who did not bother to ask his mother why she summoned (Aisha) in light of these difficult circumstances that (Ibtisam) is going through.

Although this urgent desire, striking deep in the mind of Mrs. (Salma), stems originally from her excessive belief that (Ibtisam) needs, at this particular time, a divine miracle in order to escape from the clutches of this difficult disease.

Therefore, all those close to her must participate in extending a helping hand to her, as she is the one who needs every point of hope with which to narrate all parts of her life, which gradually began to turn into a desert.

Modern medicine has no choice but to remove the diseased liver as a radical treatment, through another transplant.

It is very important and necessary for her slender body to receive the new liver and be satisfied with its presence. It is the hope that everyone awaits with supplication.

Will her body reject this strange intruder? Just as her mind resists her heart in its overflowing feelings toward her lover (Azzam).

It is love that has clear features like the rays of the morning sun on her psychological state without arguing between the thoughts of all those around her.

And the attempt to reject this love stems from a difference in ideas and not for another reason. (Hisham) was listening to the information that his mother gave him moments ago, and he felt that it was shocking and frightening.

Here, the son felt that the whole issue was related to everyone surrounding the sick (Ibtisam), and his mother had no right to choose whom she wanted from among them.

So he dares and asks her: (Aren't we supposed to present these facts in front of (Azzam), because he may live now and he believes that (Ibtisam) has found him not suitable for her, and she decided to stay away from him as a method that meets the aspirations of her intellectual inclinations, which he rejects, and in his humble opinion that he has the right to tell him about the ordeal.

And now who knows, perhaps his love for her has turned into a great hatred that will destroy her life before his life.

His mother (Salma) did not encourage this desire despite her factual evidence. Rather, she saw that telling (Aisha) was more impactful than this request at this time, especially since she had made a promise to her friend (Ibtisam) not to tell (Azzam) anything about her health.

Here the conversation moved directly to a question; perhaps the time was not to allow it, so (Hisham) said: ("Mom, what do you think now about (Aisha)?") So the caring Mother (Salma) smiled and invited him to watch the story, and in her heart a heartbeat that could not stop following the health of (Ibtisam), her preoccupation.

And she will start from tomorrow immediately inquiring about the subject of her travel and the hospital that is likely to receive those who suffer like her sick condition.

And in one of the important life turns in the journey of (Ibtisam's) illness, and after her movement and presence decreased, as well as the hours of her appearance to people, it happened that some of her lovers leaked evidence that she was ill.

And things almost hurt her from grief because she does not want anyone else to worry about her health and the developments of her illness.

On a miserable spring night when the full moon illuminates the darkness of the courtyard of the house with all the meaning of these words.

It happened that she was visited by a man whom she had previously lavished with a lot of charitable aid. This man was advancing slowly across the yard, wearing a blue hat and holding a brown rosary in his hand.

When he approached the door, he began to ring the bell. The maid heard it, so she went to open it. Her face had some expressions of apprehension and fear. He was an obedient master.

It seemed to her the majestic of the body with its hugeness and its wide black eyes with a sparkle that paralyzes the tongue and freezes movement at first sight.

He asked to meet (Ibtisam), and the maid entered him after obtaining permission from Ibtisam's mother.

She received him with her well-known welcome and he begged her to grant him a favor that he hoped (God) would help him with.

And when she found out that he wanted to donate a part of his liver to her, she could not prevent her eyes from bleeding tears, which necessitated the rising voice of her sobbing, so her poor mother intervened when she found her in this condition.

Feelings suddenly flared up in her speech, and she apologized to the poor, shy man, who, in turn, was shocked, so he decided to apologize to them, and he never intended to hurt her with his desire.

Soon, he asked their permission to leave immediately, and the maid accompanied him, and the Mother began to hold back her daughter's tears with difficulty, and the wailing was still stable in her chest.

Her only concern is the ability to calm down (Ibtisam), who seemed to be affected by the desire of the poor, kind man who exceeded every human imagination that rarely exists in this time, so who moved this desire in him?

The Mother (Fatima) was patting her daughter's collapsed shoulder in front of her broken eyes. It was tenderness, so she began to rock her and said with a smile:

("Your effort has not been in vain, my love, the good are grateful for your beautiful deed, and the love of people is the true wealth that is not granted except to the special among the servants of (Allah).")

And before the man came out, he stood and turned around. He started talking to the maid, saying to her while he swore the most sincere faith:

("Please inform Mrs. (Ibtisam) that I am serious about my offer, and that I pray to (God) to bless her with abundant health and wellness, and to protect her from the evil of this disease, and that she return to us with her gentle smile to enjoy our lives with her presence among us.")

He also asked her to tell her to strive to realize the healing while they are with her, and (God) above them is a witness to every word he uttered.

The man's visit had a heavy impact on (Ibtisam's) heart. She did not imagine that love would reach people at this important juncture in her life.

Indeed, (Allah) was completely satisfied with it. This satisfaction was represented in giving her hearts with such purity and sacrifice. that pushes a stranger to cut off a part of his body and gives it to her willingly; so that you live and continue to give humanity.

Despite the difficult health situation and the constantly growing pains, sometimes excruciating and tiring her skinny body thirsting for rest, fortunately for her, the disease did not come to the intelligence (Ibtisam).

Who realized, since her friend (Aisha) came to her, that her intentions were sound this time, and there was no doubt about all the feelings she revealed with her flaming expressions.

Ideas come successively to Ibtisam's mind, and she does not stop observing the feelings of her friend (Aisha), as she confirms that she is indeed sincere in her feelings about her illness.

It seems that she had taken from the heritage of her lightness in the days of childhood, and she remained distinguished in her presence by telling the funny stories that brought them together. Perhaps, by her actions, she is trying to raise the spirits of her gentle, broken friend, according to her point of view.

They are the memories from the time of classmates, the old teachers, the harassment on the way, and the play between the paths in the alleys.

Certainly, her supreme and convincing goal is to add a magical touch to her presence, and the torrent of these stories was only interrupted by the presence of Mrs. (Salma), alone or accompanied by her son (Hisham), whose features seemed to have abandoned the first impression on the day he saw (Aisha) for the first time at a party. Christmas.

While (Aisha) did not show him any passion or impulse toward him throughout the period, it became certain for (Ibtisam) according to what she thinks that (Hisham) at the beginning of the acquaintance had tried to find in her a reason to approach her.

Considering that she and (Ibtisam) may be similar in many characteristics since he started talking to her at the aforementioned party.

But (Aisha), unfortunately, at the time, did not present herself to (Hisham) as she should and in a manner satisfactory to his ambitions, so that he would remain confused about his matter until this moment, for which he would pay the price.

Now perhaps the look has changed, and Aisha seemed more sober, which made him look at her with amazed looks when he saw her, and she was completely different from the first days.

It seems that the tragedy of (Ibtisam's) illness or any other human tragedy is what imbues people with a mood of wisdom when they rush to reality.

Illness in such circumstances nullifies people's certainty in the adornments of life and its pleasures and makes them strive sincerely to highlight the essence of their existence and the usefulness of their life with its sweetness and bitterness, as the matter is the same!

Also, on the other hand, it seems that the veiled verbal message arrived quickly and clearly, quickly illuminating the lost soul of (Aisha), to finally land on the branches of true friendship.

Throughout that period, she had never imagined that she would love her friend (Ibtisam) to such an extent that, from that crucial moment on, she controlled her feelings and now made her forget everything.

In fact, she intentionally forgets the events of the past to be present only for the sake of her friend, who is dearer to herself and even more precious to her heart than her being.

And she never thought in the same way as before, especially when she forgot that she was there, and she kept presenting herself in blatant flattery, perhaps she could draw (Hisham's) attention to her and that he would bypass (Ibtisam), who was sitting at the time in a semi-distraction, almost not hearing what was going on around her. with her dreams.

These beautiful new meanings were seeping slowly like the morning dew into the mind of Mrs. (Salma) on the one hand and, on the other hand, stirring the feelings of (Hisham).

It is certain that Hisham, this gentle young man looking for stability, has glimpsed a positive look from his mother, inviting him to think again carefully about (Aisha) in her new dress of good morals.

While (Hisham) was thinking more comprehensively about the current circumstances, which were successive events, he felt that the time had come to re-document his desire from merely expressing a fleeting opinion with simple feelings until he actually reached what was severed from the cord of feelings with (Aisha).

But at the same time, he was also thinking of giving her life, which was covered by her friend's illness, a point of light that would create a mood of optimism.

In her belief that perhaps if he had announced now that he and (Aisha) would be engaged, this beautiful news would have been reflected in the life of (Ibtisam).

And this good news full of joy will give her positive energy to help her overcome the troubles of the disease and overcome its dangerous stage.

Thus, as soon as (Hisham) stated his desire, his mother (Salma) did not wait, so she took a corner with (Aisha) away from the scene and spoke to her directly about her son's desire to marry her.

She did so without mentioning his purpose in this advertisement now, so that she would not think that his proposal to marry her was not for her sake but rather to add a glimmer of hope with a spectrum that radiates a light of joy on the life of (Ibtisam), which was exhausted by the disease.

It is surprising and strange that (Aisha) agreed immediately, but it was also shocking what Aisha thought of on behalf of Mrs. (Salma) and her son, (Hisham).

She went jogging to Ibtisam's room and entered it to tell her the news with the intention of making her happy in these difficult moments, and everyone is closely following what this friend is doing.

To be honest, Ibtisam's smile showed the radiance that fatigue extinguished her charm, and confusion appeared in all its stereotypical forms embodied on her face.

Rather, it seemed as if she had not lived through this bitter experience and had never been ill.

Ahlam's fast travel was very painful and would have contributed to shattering the dreams of her sick sister, and this is what her mother did not wish Ahlam to do.

Obsessions began to manipulate her thoughts as she watched the condition of her daughter (Ibtisam), whose feelings began to get tense, and she was afraid to interpret travel in ways that would make the situation more complicated than it is.

However, (Ahlam) kept following her sister's condition after her travel, as Ibtisam sought an excuse for her, as her son is still young and needs her.

Her mother's arguments about accompanying her on her treatment journey became intolerable beyond all logical possibility.

How pity she was for her and her health, and for the excruciating anxieties on such tiring journeys.

Therefore, from her point of view, it is impossible for her to travel alone without an escort, and there must be someone to help her, and her friend (Aisha) may be the closest choice.

But even this desire remained in complete darkness, missing the light of reality. She did not find the blessing of her mother, nor even the encouragement of Mrs. Salma. The resounding surprise was that Mrs. Salma had completed the procedures for their travel together and that she would certainly not back down from her desire for any reason.

In turn, (Ibtisam) expressed great gratitude befitting the virtuous position of her president, who did not leave her since the disease settled in her body, and now she is preparing to accompany her to travel, and her financial deposits were not a reason to hinder the achievement of the treatment journey, despite her admission through contact with the medical departments that the transplantation of the new liver would be expensive and it will take an indefinite amount of time.

While an idea came to Ibtisam's imagination, she quickly implemented it, as she saw that, as long as Mrs. (Salma) is the one who will accompany her, there is nothing less than recommending that the marriage of (Aisha) to (Hisham) take place quickly.

The emotional atmosphere between them is charged with mutual feelings and longings, and this will be the last thing that can be touched of the happiness that everyone needs, and investing in the wedding as a driving force will invite everyone to optimism and live in overwhelming joy.

Ibtisam's request was not difficult to achieve and needed time to implement, but in her extended speech she acknowledged that Mrs. Salma's house would be the most suitable place for marriage, especially in the early days, so that her son (Hisham) can equip a suitable marital home for him and his near-future wife (Aisha).

When (Aisha) heard from Mrs. (Salma) this urgent desire, her voice over the phone immediately sounded a little confused with the intensity of joy.

Her response was immediate when she realized that it was a sincere wish from her dear friend (Ibtisam), as it was the last happy event before the date of travel.

On the other hand, it seems that (Hisham), in turn, seemed ready for a step that was the most beautiful in his life, and in this way, its events developed easily, and fate pushed the wheel of its implementation with all force.

The hesitation about accomplishing this matter would be painful if (God) had not destined their friend (Ibtisam) to recover from her illnesses that ravage her weak body.

Immediately, Ibtisam realized the true meaning of happiness when she accepts and removes the traces of sadness, despite the unbearable double pain that she feels from time to time and inside her the fires of worries that burn her wounds severely.

Fatigue was excluded from the account of this joyful day, in which joy gathered both (Aisha) and (Hisham).

Behold, the joy shone on the faces of those who were invited to the beautiful yet limited celebration.

As (Ibtisam) wanted, Mrs. (Salma) lived with her within the walls of their house, and she left her home to her son (Hisham) and (Aisha) so that they could freely prepare the marital nest, dreaming and planning for their future.

The wishes were finally fulfilled after a long wait, but at this time what was going on in the mind and heart of (Ibtisam), despite this huge amount of simultaneous events and her resorting to adopting drowning in life as a path to oblivion.

In the days preceding the trip, joy began to fill the corners of her life, despite the appearance of some fatigue on her face and the change of her features from time to time. Likewise, the signs of glad tidings began to be uttered in all directions, and on the other side was (Ahlam) through her daily contacts; It seems as if she lives with her sister and has not traveled for a moment and has not been away from her.

On the other hand, it seems that (Hisham), in turn, seemed ready for a step that was the most beautiful in his life, and in this way its events developed easily, and fate pushed the wheel of its implementation with all force.

The hesitation about accomplishing this matter would be painful if (God) did not forbid their friend (Ibtisam) to recover from the diseases that ravage her weak body.

Immediately, Ibtisam realized the true meaning of happiness when happiness comes and removes the traces of sadness, despite the unbearable double pain that she feels from time to time, and inside her the fires of worries that burn her wounds severely.

Fatigue was excluded on this joyful day, in which joy gathered both (Aisha) and (Hisham). Here is the joy shining in the faces of those who were invited to the beautiful and limited celebration at the same time.

As (Ibtisam) wanted, Mrs. (Salma) lived with her within the walls of their house, and she left her home to her son (Hisham) and (Aisha) so that they could freely prepare the marital nest, dreaming and planning for their future.

The wishes were finally fulfilled after a long wait, but at this time, what was going on in the mind and heart of (Ibtisam), despite this huge amount of simultaneous events and her resorting to adopting drowning in life as a path to oblivion.

In the days preceding the trip, joy began to fill the corners of her life, despite the appearance of some fatigue on her face and the change of her features from time to time. Likewise, the signs of glad tidings began to be uttered in all directions, and on the other side was (Ahlam) through her daily contacts; it seems as if she lives with her sister and has not traveled for a moment and has not been away from her.

Rather, she had the best help in raising and supporting her spirits because, by virtue of her being a doctor, she used to broadcast various medical advice and send some necessary instructions that would help her until the time of travel.

She thus plays the role of the sister and exercises it with perfection and devotion, a feeling that does not leave her thinking that she had left her while she was in the darkest circumstances, when she was supposed to be near her before other strangers.

Ibtisam could not bear saying goodbye to her mother in these difficult moments. The Mother quickly returned to her old features on the day her father died.

It is a state of disorientation, apprehension, and lost thoughts in the waves of fear of the unknown future.

Who knows more about the Mother (Fatima) and her personalities than her daughter? The family lived with her, including the fleeting beauty and ugliness.

It seems clear that this miserable mother from the circumstances has returned wandering with despair, and she is afraid that her sad eyes will meet the eyes of her daughter (Ibtisam), and the latter will collapse completely, but she tried with difficulty to control her emotions and give her a simple smile that suggests hope.

In a meeting with the taste of farewell before traveling, she found a demonstration of love at the entrance of their house besieging her, with a group of people from everyone who knew her at any degree of kinship.

Even the opponents, who could not understand her ideas and her ambition for the sake of others, were there to support her in her ordeal, as there is no relationship between matching ideas and standing beside the patient in his suffering.

Shock

She used to hear waves of supplication broadcast from everyone's throats, asking and pleading for her to return as if she had never been sick, sincere, and sometimes weeping prayers, which made her mute, unable to speak or comment on the great human scene.

In front of her, unprecedented and real feelings revolve.

New heroes have become an exceptional presence in (Ibtisam's) life. These events changed aspects of the world and its circumstances, and changed the scales of her thought before her heart.

What she witnessed and heard of love exceeded her ability to express, and here is the grace that makes all of these supplicate to (God) so that it may be fulfilled by the grace of healing.

It seems that there are those who extract the blessing from the time when the train of hours moves forward and refuses to stop at the stations of life so that souls can rest from the misery of circumstances.

The days passed quickly without anyone who lives in their details feeling their flow. Here it is more than a year, in which everything that indicates the love story that began as beautiful and flaming has vanished, and now it wants to end with the hand of one of its heroes haunted by a sense of accumulated shame.

(Azzam) was looking at the emptiness with eyes full of shadows of regret. He kept repeating in his mind these stabbing thoughts that were implanted in his heart and the harsh grief over his overwhelming feelings. You see that she was able to live life without him! With her heart full, she finally surrendered to her current life and took the distance on an irreversible path.

And here he wanders alone between his feelings and thoughts; questions are reflected, the majority of which center around the return of his distant sweetheart to her social class, that is far higher than his class.

Of course, this is an actual reality that cannot be denied, but she was sincere in her feelings, according to the testimony of everyone. Whoever possesses her innocence cannot be deceived or betrayed, and she belongs to her world, and she is ambitious and thinks through the framework in which she grew up from an early age.

On the morning of a rainy day, when the clock was about mid-afternoon, his friend (Hisham) visited him in the flower shop. He is the one who knows him, as he knows the lines of his palm.

He invites him to transcend his suspicious thoughts about his feelings and her feelings toward him and gives their story the meaning of life and continuity. It was certainly not a spontaneous visit; perhaps she pushed him to intervene to save their stolen love, so she loves him, so why did she prefer this silence that kills dreams?

Why does he always try to attach the error to the world in which he lives, as if there is no other positive world in it that has the most beautiful human features that contribute to giving the painting of life an attractive luster with its dazzling colors?

He was listening to his speech, which was loaded with emotions, as if he was speaking about him by proxy, revealing the thoughts of his troubled heart with his tongue.

Then why not admit for once that the recurrence of trauma made him lose confidence in finding a girl as innocent and human as (Ibtisam), or admit the bitter truth that the expansion of her life has become greater than the idea of his presence among the pages of her life written with flashy pens and picturesque of the various ideas within which there is a message good for all human beings.

It was necessary for (Ibtisam), with her great intelligence, to understand that people like (Azzam) need people who bring to their lives an amount of feelings that rain inexhaustible feelings.

In addition to their need for the flowing tenderness that takes them to the heights of pampering, greater than a person's ability to define it, especially after she heard from those who know the full story, how her difficult and painful beginnings were with orphan hood, loss, and short deprivation?

It is the events of life, nature, and destinies, when it chooses people to throw into living conditions whose gears crush their fragile souls and throw their dignity into the mud of want and need, relentlessly killing ambitions by force. Even the survivors of its wars, like (Azzam), could not take off the cloak of misery from his thinking.

It was easy for this miserable, hopeless lover to oppress her, despite what she was sending him from her clear eyes of the great ray of love.

It is a feeling mixed with a lot of sympathy, pity, and appreciation, while he practiced condescension over her the day she told him about her new activity, which she formulated herself and moved in with her boss, Mrs. Salma, while she was pushing her to the arena of good steadfastly and deliberately with wise mental actions.

Not only did he listen to her in cold impartiality but he also produced evidence of his disdain and underestimation of all the ideas she was offering him, confirming that he has wished for a role model similar to her as a child; perhaps at that time he could complete his education and remain next to his mother and sister and automatically forget the idea of leaving alone behind for a living.

The bell of those days, months, and years is still ringing, reminding him of the conditions of misery, where fatigue is a dear companion who should never be betrayed or underestimated.

That period in which Azzam faced the storms of hardships alone while he was fighting, while his mother did not sacrifice herself for him and for his weak orphan little sister, it is the world whose cruelty was manifested in these distant cities.

(Azzam) was weak, so he voluntarily surrendered to the pressures of his grief from the world and surrendered the rudder of his life boat to the waves that threw him wherever they wanted on the shore of joy, in which he is rarely present.

Perhaps he never saw that in this life there was a model similar to (Ibtisam) in her morals, her great humanity, and her good spirit, but she impersonated cruelty and was able for nearly a year to leave him alone, sipping the bitterness of his thoughts and concerns, and for him she is no different from the rest of the cruel people.

And he, despite everything, lacks courage! That is when he decided to move away for fear of being broken as a man by her decision, and when it came against his great love that he carried for her since he saw her for the first time through her apparent intransigence, and she wanted his soul to design for her a bouquet worthy of admiration. Even if it was by force, she just wanted it!

In the midst of these waves of reckless suspicions, Azzam recalled from the legacy of the past the page of that young man, Saif, who was a partner in his old torments.

Events crystallized clearly on the day he left his mother's house in search of a sufficient livelihood during his orphan hood and misery. Azzam remembered the address and left like a wounded bird in search of that good boy, and finally found him after a long search between the regions.

The affairs of this old friend were not more merciful than the affairs of his past, as if he was spinning in his place, never moving from his accompanying events.

He was afflicted with fatigue; his body weakened, poverty exhausted him, and his facial features changed.

Especially after he lost his leg in one of the town's factories. As for the strange thing about this visit, he did not find a sufficient welcome from (Saif), so he decided to throw an envelope containing some money in order to help him.

What is confusing is that he referred to the fact that there is someone who takes care of his aid, and he certainly does not need anything from anyone else, even if this person is his friend (Azzam).

It was not easy after all these years for him to break into the life of one of his past comrades and appear as fate written in the guise of a person who suddenly wanted to help his friend.

Here, he became apprehensive about the condition of his old friend, so he started to talk to him in the hope of relieving him of some of his misery, but when he initiated the question: ("Who is helping you?") He did not comment on Saif's answer with any word that silenced him completely.

Rather, he told him confidently that they are the kind young woman (Ibtisam) and the kind lady (Salma).

It is that beautiful name and that wonderful spectrum that haunts the imagination of (Azzam) day and night, pushing him to regret and despair and admonish himself without mercy for having succumbed to his fear and his cruel refusal to respond to his mind to his heartbeat for the sake of her wild love.

How easy it was for him, in a moment of despicable weakness, to forget the day her eyes told him that he was the most important man in her life without a rival.

But what shocked him and shattered his pride when he said to him: ("The financial assistance no longer comes to me with the young woman (Ibtisam), as she used to visit me and sit with me and have a good time in the company of Mrs. (Salma).")

And I have heard that she has gone abroad, and there are those who claim that she is not well. Then he begins to cry fervently for her condition and forgets his own condition at this moment.

Those quick, successive sentences were like a devastating hurricane for every glimmer of joy waiting to happen, so the sparkle of hope quickly extinguished. Here (Azzam) went in his straying, a revolutionary moment that changed the course of events.

He rushed out of the room of the friend of the past struggle (Saif); everything in it does not bode well; its pillars are inhabited by poverty and covered by dark curtains of worries hanging in the looks of his friend.

He left with his head bowed without uttering a word of farewell, hoping to return again one day, which angered him and toppled his psyche.

Did she really leave? And joined her married sister abroad when she despaired of the stagnation of the situation with her lover, or at the most difficult possibility, why did he say that (Ibtisam) was not well?

It seems that there is a mystery in the matter, and it must be deciphered immediately.

On the evening of that fateful day, he did not return home. He had to make sure of the matter with a visit that could not be postponed to (Hisham) because he is the only one who has the whole truth regarding the developments in (Ibtisam's) life, if there were developments, and in anticipation of any new, he tried immediately, called him and found his phone switched off.

Events follow in his mind, and he decides to pass by the house of Mrs. (Salma). The absent lights were a harbinger of bad luck and misfortune. He stood for moments waiting for the emptiness to surround him while he was in worrying confusion, but the reality is that none of the people of the house are here.

Fear almost kills him out of apprehension, while he suffers from that pressing and escalating feeling of confusion and distrust, trying to search for the hidden truth, and he too has been lost between the islands of ratification and the islands of denial.

(Azzam) had only one wish dearer to him than to see (Ibtisam) the love in his eyes accompanied by his fear for her, a fear that no one can imagine.

The clouds of mist disappeared from his eyes, so that the buds of truth would blossom as fate had created them, without any tampering mentioned by the hands of humans or others.

So he began to conjure his Lord with human grievances, beseeching Him and asking Him to help her in her sick ordeal. It had leaked to him from (Saif) a colleague of the past that she was sick or almost. He was asking with passion and curiosity who this (Ibtisam) was, in order for her illness to turn his entire life into a barren patch of sadness and anxiety about her health and her life together.

Rather, in addition to all those falling feelings of grief, he visits his friend (Rashid), who lives close to his beloved's house.

The alley was, as it seemed to him, from the focus of the vision, disturbed, as sadness seemed to hang over the few faces he saw at the first sight, so there was no noise; only the wide spread feeling, accompanied by the drawn anxiety, was the weather of sorrows dominating the details of the neighborhood and its people.

After saluting and asking about conditions in their general and private forms, as was the case with social customs, (Azzam) did not ask the man questions about the secret of sadness that controls the people of the neighborhood, but he tried to infiltrate his conversation with caution by touching on topics far from the life of (Ibtisam). He was waiting for opportunities to pounce, and he was pleased when her biography came.

Why the delay in asking the direct question to inquire about the condition of (Ibtisam)? The motives may be logical due to his shyness that some interpret as meddling in the affairs of others.

Or the other fundamental reason may be the possibility that Rashid's response will be unexpected and that Rashid will launch a sudden attack on him directly, knowing of her sad story with him and his injustice to her.

The friend (Rashid) was nothing but a long rambling in his speech, as if he was talking about the warm, tender, rising sun before it sets.

He said spontaneously and in a voice full of emotion: ("I don't know where to start for you, my friend, the conversations about this good neighbor (Ibtisam).")

In fact, I knew from one of the neighbors in the neighborhood that she was not feeling well, and unfortunately, she suffers from a very serious illness that may cost her her life, God forbid.

Despite (Azzam's) certainty about his beloved (Ibtisam) and her kindness, he was struck by an overwhelming feeling of astonishment. He began to wonder to himself, repeating the phrases that came out of his thoughts, so he said in a whisper: *("Which (Ibtisam) is this whose illness makes people in that form of insomnia?")*

("What is the reason for people's interest in her life while I am the last to know?")

But apparently, from the presence of her name, this friend does not know anything about the details of her illness. Perhaps the most distant circles do not realize that she is very ill, and in his belief, only those who are close to her know the whole story, and when he referred to (Azzam), the shocking answer was it is her and no one else.

(Azzam), with all his experience, could not contain the raging feelings of sadness that flared up as a result of a human condition that was clearly evident due to the illness of a girl who was not normal in any way.

His life turned into poisonous winds that uprooted all green and dry land from the shores of his dreams. Hope sometimes came to tickle his feelings, giving her an impetus of optimism that she would return to him, even if it took a long time and the faces of those around her life changed.

Little news was known about her being created for unlimited benevolence and giving, so he was not surprised by the presence of the names (Ibtisam) and Mrs. (Salma) in one sentence, as if they lived in one body, exchanging roles in the lives of poor people in need of these pure souls.

Despair overwhelmed (Azzam), who was shocked by the last details and developments, and in the heart of which was the news of the illness of his beloved (Ibtisam), which cut him into two opposing halves, one of which blames the other ferociously the grieving lover.

He quickly went to his e-mail, wishing to send her a long, groaning message, not knowing to whom he wanted to reach.

He met in her estrangement what shattered him completely and planted fatal grievances in his chest.

Dear Ibtisam,

It is not easy, or so I thought life is, when the word I love you comes from the heart of a man in the circumstances of my life toward a girl who is living in the early spring. He is in a real emotional crisis.

Perhaps the spaces of joy widened to make just a simple, spontaneous word, or a sign directed to you, an opportunity for a girl of such beauty, confidence, and tenderness to enter my life.

I had to tell you more about my life than my tragic details; the events of which those close to you plotted, without looking into the things and wisdom behind them, or telling you about my beautiful torment and my estrangement between the folds of your kindness that always captivates hearts.

Nothing settles in front of my will, and there are no achievable dreams to the extent of my sad experience with the nature of things and my absurd struggle with the movement of fates, but with you, I was moving behind my feelings like a bird on the branches, bouncing freely with my feelings.

On the day of the flower shop incident, everyone seemed like a mirage of their imagination, and the world had disappeared. until it appears as a cloud of smoke, and only your soul fills the place, so I used to blame my soul for making you rob it and leave for your innocent and gentle worlds, away from all that I know of trifles and meaningless noises, and when I stumbled upon you, I realized that my fortunes abandoned their shadows and headed toward the bright future of your countenance.

And (Azzam) began to refute those moments in detail and accurately narrate their details, remembering them when they sat in that exceptional winter inside that luxurious restaurant.

At that time, he was an innocent teenager, practicing in his imagination an intimate embrace with all its details, but it was discipline, permissible dreaming, and the grace of imagination that it is necessary for the deprived to prostrate for eternity in order to thank God's providence for it.

He told her that it would be an honor for them to admit their defeats in public; in order for those we love to benefit from it, for the first time he sees himself shaken in choosing the right and wise decision, and he really wants to shout to her at the top of his voice in front of the public saying (I love you) simply, but unfortunately he cannot.

So where is she now, and where is he? She has become like a light butterfly that does not tread on the ground and does not burn in the presence of the light.

He informs her that until this moment he does not believe that the year is nearing an end, as they may continue together or separate together, and they are unable to find a clear name for their feelings. She is the young girl looking for the missing father who was suddenly absent, or does she want that lover who seemed to be infatuated with her to the point of intoxication?

Both of them are looking for an unknown that will not come, and reality denies his presence. They are looking for painkillers that are more decisive than the regular ones that stop the pain for a few minutes, but they are certain that they will still be sick with an incurable disease that (Azzam) considers the ideal scientist who restores the kingdom of their love. With Ibtisam, he believes that he has found it.

Time scrambled for their fate, and he had to admit that what he said would make him feel complete psychological comfort, as he loves her as an exceptional case and as a friend present in the course of his current and upcoming life, and there is no escape or place in the world that he can turn to in order to live as a refugee from the tyranny of her love, which has become a reality haunting his sleep.

And he will not forget her gesture, which he did not think was spontaneous at the time, when she said to him with a smile: ("I was waiting for your call so that you would exercise on me the anxiety of a father who wanted to be reassured that I was in my bed.")

However, he ignored this sentence, which was full of the word (father), and he could not analyze it before it was lost between the rest of the sentences of the meeting that brought together their feelings in the light of candles and the melodies of romantic music that added a dramatic plot that did not and will not end.

To be honest, he also confessed how much he wished to live the role of the human father and practice his images full of strong emotions, so passion seized him, and he was amazed at the desire lurking inside him as it was approaching him little by little.

He is practicing psychological discipline to the point of terror while they are walking in the garden attached to the restaurant; her lips are silent, and her eyes are always looking at his smiling face.

And he completes that expressive message that while he was with her, it was necessary for him to fall into romance like a dreamer in order to step into reality for the first time in his miserable life, and the girl who loved him found herself in the aftermath of a bad choice, and she recklessly wanted to defeat time, and she is sure that time cannot be defeated by personal decision.

Is it possible here for (Azzam) to imitate the position of the honest advisor in such volatile circumstances and simply invite her, pleading that she overcome the ordeal, considering it as a symptom of false rain?

And does he admit his defeat to the calculations of time and distance and accuse her of coming late to enter the arena of his life, which is full of wounds that are still burning despite the passage of many years of its inception?

In his heart, he sees that nothing is working anymore, the birds have left their nests and left him to tinker with circumstances, so he admits that she is far away because she is sick, so he feels that the world has poured a beaker of ice water on his sleeping soul in a deep slumber that does not want to get up from his daydreams at all.

It is the full and voluntary confession with a bitter burning in his chest that unfortunately he did not feel the depth of her absence. He also did not feel the long distances between their bodies and their souls, except when she was sitting in the distance, as she was in pain and ignited in his life, his life, his thought, and his broken heart with the fires of separation, and only her velvet whispers extinguished it.

He adds in the letter that he remembers how much greater she was than him in thought and feelings and had tremendous energy to produce love in a way greater than his poor fantasies. She is the one who formed his first impression of her through that great aura of presence and the seismic effect of the smile that is manifested as an overflow, with the two dimples that make her cheeks a gift from the generous and merciful God for the unfortunate and the grieving.

He also admits that in this fateful message for his life, and after much trouble adapting to the situation with its sweet and bitter details, he clearly learned from her how to dare and not leave his fear for her if she is absent from him again in similar circumstances in the future.

He was still touching on the last meeting that brought their hearts together before she disappeared. He had discerned the desire for her to tell him something other than what she said.

He thinks that the words emanating from the eyes are greater and deeper than what their tongues say. Another phantom was moving toward him, throwing herself in his arms, so he remained silent and almost did not hear her, preoccupied with astonishment, he did not believe himself that it was her, he did not believe that the fates finally sympathized and gave him her love.

And it is that love. And what does this overwhelming human emotion mean to them other than an attempt to complete it like a crescent?

It is his birth, then it grows and expands until it becomes a full moon and illuminates the darkness of loneliness and gives the night a light that radiates on the foreheads of lovers.

At the end of his letter, Azzam says that he is not a racist because he did not find perfection before he met her pure soul, so he lacked something, and in her absence he realized how great he had lost, so he advises her and begs her not to be defeated in the face of illness.

Not a victory for her life, but because it will lead to his certain death if he wakes up one day and does not find her in his world, that is why he will pray for her to return; otherwise woe to him!

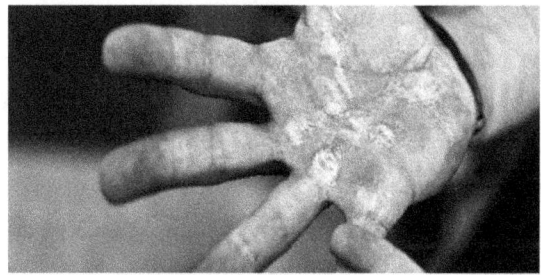

I put dyes in my palms; maybe he sees it and grabs it!
They are only his colors, but his fingers are mine!

Salvation

(Ibtisam) realized that there is nothing in a person's life more difficult than waiting for relief for his health crisis; until this moment, no good news has arrived about the presence of a donor, and time passes and her condition sometimes gets worse and at other times stabilizes, the only thing that was positive in the hospital was the continuous talk With Mrs. (Salma), even staying in her own room was very time-consuming.

She seemed optimistic despite the absence of evidence that Ibtisam would soon end her suffering from psychological fatigue before physical fatigue, especially since time is not in favor of the pathological condition that her weak body has reached. Her fear stems from her condition getting worse over time and developing into something bigger than the liver itself.

While (Ibtisam) kept peeping whenever she had the opportunity to see how Mrs. (Salma) reacts to the rushing hours of time.

Since she came here, she has realized that her virtuous president is too patriotic to put into words.

It seems that she cannot bear the idea of being separated from her family or her work, but she remained faithful to help (Ibtisam) pass through that difficult and worrisome test in the full sense of the word.

She also realized that it was kindly destinies that made this noble lady to be next to her in that difficult human circumstance.

But on the other side of waiting, she was hoping that something from (Azzam) would reach her. Despite her insistence on concealing the news of her illness so as not to affect the form of the relationship.

Bewilderment crept into the shores of her calmness in order to know where the love story had reached. Perhaps a happy new thing will happen if she rises from her malaise, and it seems that the issue of longing to hear upcoming news indicates that (Azzam) is still keen, or, to be precise, he has come out of his isolation and reached a decision concerning her and wants to contact her.

Thinking of him has become the preoccupation that sometimes makes her forget the pain of the disease. The absence and separation have long affected her tender heart, which is still beating until this moment with the letters of his name.

What brings out melodies resounding in her mind in order for her to sleep in the stillness of wandering accompanied by dreams is the longing to see him or to hear his latest news at the very least, so when will the wishes and suspicions be fulfilled in the ideas that build their nests?

She regrets that there was no one to give her any indication that (Azzam), this strange lover, by a blind fateful coincidence, knew that the past year, which witnessed her parting from him, was carrying out her charitable activities in the company of the great lady (Salma), her companion and confidant of her secrets.

The days were spent in humanitarian activities with the official (Salma). For her, these charitable activities contributed to healing the wounds of separation that (Azzam) caused her. This lover, with his strange behavior, issued judgments without investigating the facts.

But in the end, things turned out to be more cruel than he thought. The fact that the sun of reality does not lose sight of is that Mrs. (Salma) is still concealing the matter of the important and fateful message in the life of the sick (Ibtisam). Rather, her son (Hisham) dared himself and sent a short message encouraging (Ibtisam) to open her personal mail in order to read (Azzam's) letter to her, but his mother leaves no room for this wish to be fulfilled at all at the present time.

And because she was not able to accomplish this simple work, and also out of her excessive confidence in Mrs. (Salma), she was inviting her to follow up on her personal mail and, in turn, informing her of the important content of these messages.

Unfortunately, she never touched on (Azzam's) message, which seemed to have reached an impressive amount to the point that even she could not bear it, and she felt the strength of what he wrote of sincere expressions that made the stone cry.

So Mrs. (Salma) was not keen on conveying the content of the letter of apology to (Ibtisam), but for honesty and honesty when she recited the text to her after the pressure and insistence exerted on her by her son (Hisham), who appeared from his matter indicating that (Azzam) had finally reached him, and it seemed he has signs of psychological fatigue and an exhausted body.

After (Azzam) found out about the developments of (Ibtisam's) illness, he told him that he had written her a letter of apology and how much he wished that she would read it, and as his mother (Salma) bet on her reaction, as soon as she finished reading the letter; until she found happiness inhabited by grief, manifested on her face, and signs of satisfaction sweeping across her features, which changed automatically, and her face shone like the moon.

He was very successful in choosing the words of his message, and the expressions in it are melancholy, touching the heart, so that he gets lost among its vocabulary full of feelings. Believing that she has outgrown him, she no longer loves him and has entered her new life, a life in which he has no place.

After a few seconds of silence and distraction with memories, Mrs. (Salma) did not want to pressure (Ibtisam), who seemed very affected by what she heard. There the worried girl started recounting to her the memories of that day in which she spoke in her own way, so that she would make him feel that he was the most important thing to her in this world.

Just before sunset on a day that seemed cold, she stopped her car in front of the flower shop, and fear besieged her as she fought it.

He did not feel her presence while he was looking at the world from behind the thick glass, casting his broken looks at a group of young men and women sitting on the sidewalk opposite the store. Their movements and laughter suggest to the observer that they own their lives and freedom.

Rather, they are indifferent and interested in the looks sent to them from those around them; who keeps looking at them all the time, it seems that their only dream is for the world to bring them together under a roof of love.

Ibtisam did not want to invade his privacy at this time, so she decided to leave immediately. Confusion settled on the shores of her thoughts between going to him and not giving in to her desire to talk to him.

So she sat looking in silence, but fortunately she recorded his house address, which Hisham gave her without hesitation, and without apprehension she decided to visit him at his house this evening.

She does not know how long it will take until he hears the doorbell, as it seems that he is not accustomed to being visited by anyone in his house. Some ideas come and disappear to reveal new ideas that cancel out the previous ones. Suspicions are sometimes very harsh on the hearts of lovers. She soon smiled as she stopped her car in front of His house. She went down walking with her legs heavy and her body shivering in cold or fear; she doesn't know; everything is linked to his reactions.

Here she is, standing firmly in front of the door as much as possible. She rang the bell, so he opened it quickly. From the inside, her features were not clear. His gaze betrayed him, but her voice said that it was her. Shyness pervaded all its details. The life of a single man does not suggest a greater bet than a bet on meeting chaos, but he quickly closed his door. He found her violently leaning toward his lap and weeping bitterly, bridging his tongue.

His feelings were neutral, and he remained motionless out of astonishment and did not know the reason. Was it surprise, boldness, or fear that seemed to spread his soldiers to occupy his thoughts, but suddenly he put his trembling hand on her shoulder, calming her down and relieving the stress of the meeting. After all this distance, he promises her that there will be no new separation.

She sat for minutes, sighing in her chest, the conversations of the two lovers crowded, wanting to leave, so she moved her clear, weeping eyes in all corners, and she saw the books lying scattered around and the computer emitting quiet, dreamy music that steals the hearts; he was running it in a whisper while he was lying on the black couch, apparently trying to search in files, he does not know what is in them; perhaps it was a game of silence, or his patience is running out.

He seemed to want to sit more comfortably. He had not slept for the past three days. He was tossing and turning in his bed, struggling with his worries. A lot of fatigue and pallor appeared on his features. Black color was drawn around his eyes.

So he lay down like a child, sleeping almost in the middle of the sofa, with some pillows facing the green wall at the back of his head.

And she, in turn, is sitting to his right, still contemplating the details of his apartment. She asked him about that large white bag that rests on an old brown wooden table.

His response came as a shocker, by all means, confusing her calmness. He said to her in a miserable, desperate voice: (In the bag is my shroud, which I bought some time ago so that there would not be a great commotion on the day of my death.

He continued his speech with an orphan tear burning in his eyes, so he told her that people would find everything in the process of being prepared. The answer shocked her, so she rushed to throw herself on the largest possible area of his chest, then she in turn began to cry. While (Azzam) did not rise to this spontaneous behavior from her, it seemed as if He needed that despite his good intentions in this humanitarian scene.

His heart was beating violently and at an unusual speed, as if he was a teenager being seduced by an experienced female who was playing with his feelings. She even felt these accelerated beats and told him about them.

But he answered an answer that changed the form of her body movement, which became just leaning on his chest, and his body was still in the same form, without movement or emotion, like a boulder, a motionless, deaf stone.

There was no speech but silence on the lips, no reproach for any degree of cruelty, and no intimation was exerted on him equivalent to the form in which she settled in his bosom.

Soon, she calmed down and began to close her eyes, wanting to recall all the dreams of this time in the life of their love story.

She felt the extent of her need at this defining moment in her life, which was marred by repulsion without a convincing reason to condemn it.

In the abstract, she is only an insomniac girl who found the perfect space to help her get a peaceful sleep after a long suffering and continuous struggle with insomnia that disturbs loving hearts.

Thus, she stopped talking at once. It was that silence that really made him believe that she had fallen asleep, and his heartbeat returned to calm.

Without a possible warning, the fingers of his hand quickly took the initiative, slipping through the locks of her hair at times, patting her shoulder at times, and whispering to her to be reassured, as silence in such situations is what hearts desire.

He is only afraid of losing her, as the miserable days he went through away from her are enough for him.

Minutes later, they got up from their place together as a single mess. He was aware that her passion pushed her to ask many questions. She tried to return to a chair that came directly in front of him, but she could not.

So, she sat almost beside him, looking at him again, smiling, and in her eyes a ray of light was evident, and the sound of music was still emanating from all over, and he looked through the window of the room, observing the stars in the sky, perhaps he was immersed in thinking without speaking.

He was trying to choose the space that would allow her to exist, and what would happen if she was gone? But he pities her situation and her life is full of hope, in which aspirations soar and do not rest, so his sad, velvety voice kept pushing her to ask him to talk about his feelings and not his concerns.

As a matter of fact, she didn't want him to shut up, but she didn't want to get involved in confronting his negative thoughts about the whole story, but he promised her that there would be no parting after today; they had tasted his bitter taste, and they didn't deserve to drink it all the time.

Rather, the time has come for hearts to settle, souls to calm down, and a life of harmony and friendship to return to its most beautiful form, away from sorrow and pain.

As for her, she was insisting on trying to get him out of that sad weather, so she asked him to go out to the hall and turn up the music because she wanted to dance with him. He asked her if she was serious about her request.

She was afraid that it was he who could not, but with the loudness of the music, they danced together, extracting glances from him that had a thousand meanings, and when the dance ended, he embraced her and cried.

When (Ibtisam) finished narrating this situation in its most accurate details and events, she was hoping that Mrs. (Salma) did not feel it and did not hear it.

Rather, at that moment, she wanted to hug her violently in order to prove to her the extent of her love for her and to try as much as possible to play the role of a tender mother who is absent from this situation and to feel how much she needs such maternal embraces full of emotions.

She kept watching her for a few moments, and she found in front of her nothing but a wax statue that hardly moved and did not shake its eyelids.

She was looking as if unconscious, extending in her disturbing silence, taking a fixed goal from which her gaze would not deviate.

It seemed to her that she was talking to herself and that she had an overwhelming desire to talk to her, even if it was to correct some concepts. She said with a smile:

"- Oh my dear daughter, (Ibtisam).

- Love is not like life and its details. It wants us to establish a way back, ensuring that we get out of the experience without losses.

- Caution in the absolute does not prevent fate if it wants to extend its scepter."

It seems to the observer that the crisis of (Ibtisam), which has now seeped into the mind of the experienced lady (Salma), is that she has matured into the certainty of a child.

She seemed to realize the value of herself over the standards of a beautiful female, but she struggled for the victory of her humanity above all.

He (Azzam) loved her more than she thinks, but unfortunately he kept fearing for her, even for himself, because according to his point of view, he is not as innocent as hers.

With the passage of time, (Ibtisam) learned after a while that (Azzam) had visited her mother, and the strange thing is that he introduced himself to her as a friend of her daughter only, and perhaps he thought that her mother was not one of those who support the idea of his marriage to be.

If she or others were the ones who gave his girl the opportunity to stop loving him and not continue her contact with him, but he sincerely wanted to hear any news that would reassure him about her health condition, he was overwhelmed by suspicions and obsessions played with his feelings.

He did not produce expressions suggestive of his complete ignorance of (Ibtisam's) developments with the story of her illness. The greatest thing that reached her mother (Fatima) from this fleeting visit was that he controlled his features as much as he could, but his eyes were shining from suppressed tears with concern for her health.

The mother's feelings were not to be mistaken, as she is aware of those emotional human matters. She knows very well how to read people's feelings, whether they are true or false.

All she had to do was reassure him immediately and asked him to wait until (Ibtisam) returned from visiting some relatives in the neighborhood; perhaps (God) something would happen after that.

So he left her with a feeling of sadness that he could not manage, and doubt planted its daggers in his chest, so he sighed and exhaled sorrows with groans.

There was no one in front of (Azzam) available in this fog of tension except his friend (Hisham), so he went through the trouble of visiting him in his private farm and did not find him; he called him and he did not find his phone allowed, but it was closed.

On a quick visit to the bank, he clearly sensed that the friends surrounding (Ibtisam) might give him satisfactory answers without him asking, which makes him reassured of her health, at least until this moment.

After (Azzam) returned home, he found a call from (Hisham), who explained his absence because he was preparing his own marital home, and that he was now residing in his mother's house.

In this sense, it was not difficult for him to understand where Mrs. (Salma) would be now, for (Ahlam) the sister of (Ibtisam) had apparently traveled from her news with her husband, and the Mother was still residing in her house alone.

So, logically and certainly, Mrs. (Salma) is the one who accompanies (Ibtisam) on her treatment journey, despite that the news was not saturated in any case, but at the end of the call he gave Hisham an opportunity to tell (Ibtisam) when the opportunity arose to tell her that he lives with his dreams of a flower shop awaiting her; where the events of their story began and fate led them to him, so they brought them together without a date.

He also asked him to tell her that what he is doing is not for anything, and even if her love for him declines, he will remain her loyal friend who wishes her happiness and a complete recovery.

And because (Hisham) was entrusted with this request, he sent his mother a message with this meaning, a message that left a great impact on the heart of (Ibtisam).

The days of waiting were drawn by horses of patience, despite the hardness they contained on the heart of (Ibtisam), who was sick in this compulsive estrangement. And who wants (God) to find someone to donate part of his liver to her.

They are days with the taste of a full evaluation of her experience since she was a child and until the day she met the beloved (Azzam), who added dramatic scenes to her life.

She did not want to experience the meaning of that need for his presence in her life, but as she previously announced to her sister, she sees in her presence in his life the meaning of the moral commitment that he sincerely wants to extract from his circumstances, and he must trust in that meaning because it is real and honest without falsifying feelings, and was it necessary to get sick? Until he breaks the wall of his silence and acknowledges the importance of spending the coming days together.

This annoying question put many pressures on her, and it is greater than feeling the pain of the disease.

These many increasing tragedies are constantly establishing in the consciences of people the meanings of wisdom from the things that happen suddenly in their lives, lapse to change the course of things, and had it not been for hope, the world would have narrowed down for man.

Just as I became certain and believed that people like her have nothing but to seek the help of patience and wait for the near relief in its inevitable and destined forms. The experience of life and death is the same in every circumstance and time.

And how can she deny this when her family went through a realistic experience that never needs proof of its credibility. Her father was not old on the day he died and passed away, nor was her mother deserving of this worldly brokenness.

And her sister (Ahlam) is not harsh with her judgments through her feelings as long as she belongs to actual reality and lives by its conditions, even if she is sometimes unjust to all her aspirations. Ibtisam's disease is the disease of all sensitive hearts, which wants to escape from the nature of matters in which the results may be undesirable or logical for the vanquished.

And as long as she submits to the judgment of her Lord, there is nothing less than that she will go through the bitter experience to the end, whether with (Azzam) or with illness or with death itself.

For this tender young woman, things are just inevitable results in which she does not have the absolute freedom to choose as she desires, so it is wise not to torture her soul, and she did not?

Lotus bouquets.

It is also life; there is no escape from it to another world built by our dreams, and there is no other thing imposed on us without our will and consent.

The good ones are always supported by the power of faith, and with this faith establishes certainty in (God's) justice and wisdom.

It will be a long wait for Ibtisam's psyche until they find a suitable donor to put part of his liver in her body to dispel any trace of despair.

And here is the sun shining in her room, spreading warmth in its corners, and she is cheerful and patient. With her at a distance is her loving mother, who is killed by fear with obsessive weapons toward her daughter, who is dear to her heart.

And (Ibtisam) has also never renounced her moral meanings, which have become part of her personal formation. She follows the news of the humanitarian cases she is committed to and the small projects and their owners whose cases she has adopted.

And in the great test of patience that (Ibtisam) experienced with all its details, the heavens finally sympathized with her, and (God) answered the prayers of those who truly loved this good girl.

The suitable donor liver arrived, the transplant was successfully performed, she was discharged from the hospital, and she lived a long period of convalescence until things stabilized and her body recovered.

The rest of the time she was back in the hospital for follow-up before her doctor gave her the signal that she was back.

And it was those good tidings that would enlighten her life after a pervasive darkness that she did not deserve. That young woman who swore a promise and never broke it. She will help the needy as long as the spirit flows through her weak body, and only illness deters her from her actions.

Thus, after a not short period of time, the events accelerated as it was leaked to people that God had blessed (Ibtisam) with the grace of healing, so joy spread to everyone's faces and happiness spread to her opponents before her lovers, but what the good girl did not expect was that shocking scene as she walked out of the airport. Accompanied by Mrs. (Salma) on her memorable return.

The scene was so vast that she could bear it, so her feelings began to awaken her tears to overflow and drown in them, as she watched a great public reception for her that only happens to a great person or a leader, muttering in her secret: *(Oh God... all this love is for me? And what is wealth worth in front of her? This scene, this can only happen in a fantasy or a dream.)*

Circumstances prove to us the true nature of the people around us. The current feelings do not matter at all. They are human souls that are revealed only when calamities and hardships arise. From them, you see strange and sometimes suspicious actions in their funny forms.

Among them are those who flee and go away, resorting to seclusion in their cave, hiding, and among them are those who cling to each other and do not leave them, no matter how great the events are and how things change.

He contributes valiantly and sincerely to remove the expenses of eternity from our shoulders.

Then she began to follow the steps of the companion on the path, Mrs. (Salma), and she said, echoing in a whisper of thoughts, and her words spilled like a stream on her soul: *(People for people)*, that phrase clearly reflected that

(God) had answered their prayers and sincere prayers for this kind, gentle girl, and they wished her health and wellness and removed her cloud.

The people who attended this wonderful day full of their feelings almost carried her to her car, while she could hardly believe what she saw and heard of the cheers or even managed to prevent her crying, which shed tears from her eyes without her controlling them, and her mother, in turn, did not resist a feeling of elation and joy being the mother of this. The really great girl who left a trace of what makes this crowd of people go out to receive her in that hot weather.

For long hours, she was impatiently awaiting the arrival of her daughter, praying to God. The bright full moon was absent from the sky of her life, and her nights turned black and dark, so no one knew the exact time of the arrival of the plane carrying their sweetheart and their daughter.

The Mother did not stop for a moment from thinking about what would make them happy, despite all the pain she was going through.

Here, the justice of (God) becomes clear, which is consistent with her sincerity and devotion to good deeds without return to her person.

And she believed with certainty to offer a share of her humanity that would transform the lives of miserable people into another happy life, achieving as much as she could for a living without hurting their souls by applying the equation of giving in return.

The experience of the illness of the young woman (Ibtisam) would not have passed without thinking of it as an experience worthy of contemplation and reflection and benefiting from her human lessons and lessons. Rather, she made a secret vow (to God) that he would grant her a full recovery and a safe exit from the ordeal of the disease, to direct the compass of her movement and her life. For another direction, he (God) is the one who knows her Lord about his motives and his innermost being, and she calls on Him to inspire her with steadfastness to face the upcoming challenges.

Rather, she vowed in secret a sincere vow (to God), that if he grants her a complete recovery and a safe exit from the ordeal of illness, she would direct the compass of her movement and her life to another direction.

A direction to (God), who knows her motives and intrigues, and she calls on him to inspire her with steadfastness in the heart to face the upcoming challenges.

Some people's exit to receive (Ibtisam) after her return from the long treatment journey was spontaneous and innocent, but after her return, she kept repeating for a while the scene of people waiting for her return at the airport and in the area where she lives, and she tried to analyze this love, which seemed like a phenomenon that deserves a lot of consideration and contemplation of its messages and meanings.

If life in its length and breadth is not upright unless there is a dream that makes this life a meaning that is not comparable to anything else, then the stability of the dream and its lack of development may reach at some point the peaks of boredom, and a work dyed with a routine nature that does not carry a hobby of loving its continuation.

Whoever gives her life again will certainly keep her for a greater work than it was, so let her wait for the coming days and the events that the days will throw on the shores of her life.

The return of (Ibtisam) from her treatment trip carries with it a moral responsibility directed mainly to the people who were waiting for her on a huge plateau of love filled with the anxiety of waiting, in addition to the nervous fear about her return as it was, and for her health, which was subjected to this difficult and dangerous test.

To be honest, the days following her return were very difficult and caused unbearable pressures on her psyche. She will most likely need, after a while, to follow up on another journey, the developments of what happened to her, as much as the social circle closest to her was trying hard and sincerely to make this wonderful girl forget that she had A private life must be lived and not let water run through its fingers, as there is a wound that has not healed and it must be treated with courage.

It is not wise in anything for her to forget herself and abandon her previous dreams to plunge into the midst of human actions to this extent and complete obedience, as her lovers will never be satisfied that she will be crushed for their sake, so the beginning was from her mother, who confronted her for the first time with the truth of her story with the young man (Azzam), who showed a lot of his feelings the day he visited her to ask about her, despite all the behavioral precautions he showed that destroyed his soul, so as not to appear in the image of the anxious lover.

Things are starting to clear up and settle down. She must now get rid of her ambiguity and her old personal accounts, and in no way should any of the two sides of the relationship give in to their concerns about the other.

She loves him, and he reciprocates the feeling of love in the largest area, and even larger than she imagines about the truth of his sincere feelings, and this does not need overwhelming proofs to prove its usefulness from its total denial.

So what is she waiting for from him after all this time that was wasted under the pressure of unpleasant calculations, and she may see that this relationship is doomed to failure and not continuing, so she told her that the world is giving and taking, and there are no human beings on earth in the status of angels, so it is time for her to break the knot of separation with her hand and not wait from him to find his steps to her where she sits on the throne of her convictions only.

It seems that some valuable advice after the return was not only practiced by the Mother but also by her sister (Ahlam), who is always accused of being too realistic, prompting her to reconsider the issue of leaving the ball in (Azzam's) court. In order for him to win for his love for her or to get out of her life, despite the difficulty of (Ibtisam), the lover, to bear this unjust exit.

All evidence points to only one result, especially after she spoke to Mrs. (Salma) prior to the serious surgery. It is not easy for her while she faces these difficult circumstances with this much pain, so she gambles to impersonate feelings that are not real.

Love dies if (Ibtisam) goes too far with her stubbornness. She says the whole truth while she is in the hands of her Lord at a fateful moment in which there is no escape from telling the truth and nothing else.

So why does she not walk to her lover (Azzam) in the middle of the distance and try to give him hope that they are greater than any obstacles that might prevent their eternal bond, despite the unfair injustice she was subjected to by confiscating the last hope for their story, so he closed the curtain before the end of the last scene of the last chapter.

She was suspicious of his actions toward her, and his painful rejection of her stemmed from his expectation of failure and rejection when he sought to propose to her.

But on the other side of the story, she needed, in the light of her knowledge of his circumstances and his painful past, which was not without tragedy, to shower him with extreme confidence in love, which contributes to making him advance toward her while he is sure of obtaining a positive response to his request.

On a bright morning, (Azzam) found on his phone screen a message from his friend (Hisham), which was expressive to the point of calling him to get out of the circle of fear and not wait for more than this.

Indeed, it was a shame for the whole world to realize that his beloved (Ibtisam) had returned after (God) completed her with the grace of healing, and he would be the last person to know this fact.

So when, in the light of this message, he received something indicating that (Ibtisam) had really returned, he did not wait, so he returned again to send the morning bouquets of red and white lotuses, and they had an effect that seems much greater than the first days of his relationship with her.

In her turn, (Ibtisam) could not give in to the idea of waiting, especially after she got rid of the meaning of his return because she was sick, and great love turns into greater compassion.

(Azzam) was obligated, as an elegant man, to go to her, even as a way of congratulating her on her return, and she was completely cured of her illness, but inside him, he was aware that time had completely consumed him, and his life had lost a huge amount of time.

Had it not been for what happened, he would have accompanied her instead of Mrs. (Salma), so he did not find in himself the sincere desire to go as a friend only.

Rather, he imitated a strong sense of daring and set out to finally confront (Ibtisam) with his love, along with her family, with the truth of his circumstances, which would not hinder his ability to make her happy at all, as much as it led him to believe that their rejection of him was the one waiting for him in the end.

As a very important expression of that bold desire, he was preceded by lotus bouquets to the house of (Ibtisam), and in the folds of his soul he carries a precious ring with which he proposes to his girlfriend, after a long wait, a long suffering, and a long separation.

It was the features of those who received (Azzam) who helped him to get this precious ring out, and a smile of contentment clearly reflected in the morning light on (Ibtisam's) face means that he has finally returned to their abandoned nest, and that she would not have had any control over his desire to get close to her and link his life with hers other than the quick approval that it means he is the most suitable man.

He is for her the beloved, who is close to her soul and resides in her heart, and whose life would not be straight without his presence. Everyone smiled in a demonstration of love and welcome, while (Azzam) was punishing himself in secret because he had deprived himself of the blessing of being close to this pure and kind soul, and under the pretext that they would not accept him and respond to his desire to be the man of Ibtisam, whom he had always wanted as a partner for his life and dreams.

And here they are all gathered, and the most joyful one is the Mother, in her heart crying happiness whose springs do not dry up, and as for Mrs. Salma, she was speaking, and in her eyes the scenes of the bright future were evident.

As for the son (Hisham), his wife (Aisha) was sitting near him, smiling in overwhelming joy, and their eyes did not leave their happy friends.

This is the departure of suffering after a long wait, which is gone without return, to spread joy and spread the fragrance of love over the place.

There are conversations carried by the breezes of strong feelings in the hearts of everyone whose pulse is heard, and here they are exchanging looks and gestures through smiles that bestow a unique charm on the atmosphere.

(Ibtisam) was dancing to his tunes in her imagination, holding the hand of her lover (Azzam), looking into his eyes, and he was drawing his tender, captivating smile for her when their gazes intersected.

Had it not been for despair, I would not have taken hope as my path.
To you, I was a prisoner fighting my despair.

The End

www.ingramcontent.com/pod-product-compliance
Lightning Source LLC
Chambersburg PA
CBHW021853241025
34508CB00054B/2081